"I'm Not Afraid Of You."

He did another one of those slow, lingering perusals of her face and her cheeks burned under his gaze. "Maybe you should be."

Maybe he was right. Maybe she should be afraid. But she wasn't. She straightened her spine and the action closed some of the distance between them, bringing her breasts to within a micrometer of his chest.

"Maybe," she said. "But none of the Cains have power over me anymore. I've made sure of that."

Of course, that was a bald-faced lie, because if he found out the truth, then he most certainly would have power over her. A lot of it.

Dear Reader,

Usually I use this space to talk about the book you're about to read, but today I wanted to talk about something else. The people who help make my books possible—my editors.

I've written seventeen books so far, fifteen for Harlequin Books, two for other publishers. In that time I've worked with eight editors, all of whom have their own strengths and all of whom have made me a better writer. Brenda Chin bought my first book, a Harlequin Temptation. She taught me so much about how to tighten a story and layer in conflict and emotion. MJ, the editor who brought me from Temptation to Desire, eased that transition for me. She taught me how to write the big emotional, high drama stories of the Harlequin Desire line. Stacy Abrams (my editor at Walker Books) helped me refine my language and tighten up the relationships between characters. And then, there's Charles, my current editor for Desire, who is perhaps the most fun to work with. Perhaps that's because I've always felt like he really got me as a writer. Plus, he is the most fun at conferences, which makes me the envy of all my writer friends.

All of my editors have worked so hard to make my books better. I cannot imagine my life as a writer without them. Editing is so much more than merely tweaking language. Editors bring an impersonal eye to the story. They point out inconsistencies in character and story that a writer is simply too close to the story to see. They find the things we miss. They see what we cannot.

For all the editors I have worked with, as well as all the other behind-the-scenes folks, thank you!

Emily McKay

EMILY McKAY

ALL HE EVER WANTED

H HARLEQUIN®

entertain, enrich, inspire™

Recycling programs
for this product may
not exist in your area.

ISBN-13: 978-0-373-73201-2

ALL HE EVER WANTED

Books by Emily McKay

Harlequin Desire

The Tycoon's Temporary Baby #2097
**All He Ever Wanted* #2188

Silhouette Desire

Surrogate and Wife #1710
Baby on the Billionaire's Doorstep #1866
Baby Benefits #1902
Tempted Into the Tycoon's Trap #1922
In the Tycoon's Debt #1967
Affair with the Rebel Heiress #1990
Winning It All #2031
   "His Accidental Fiancée"
The Billionaire's Bridal Bid #2051
Seduced: The Unexpected Virgin #2066

**At Cain's Command*

EMILY McKAY

has been reading romance novels since she was eleven years old. Her first Harlequin Romance book came free in a box of Hefty garbage bags. She has been reading and loving romance novels ever since. She lives in Texas with her geeky husband, her two kids and too many pets. Her debut novel, *Baby, Be Mine,* was a RITA® Award finalist for Best First Book and Best Short Contemporary. She was also a 2009 *RT Book Reviews* Career Achievement nominee for Series Romance. To learn more, visit her website, www.EmilyMcKay.com.

For Brenda, Tanya, MJ, Diana, Krista, Stacy, Michelle, and—perhaps most important!—Charles. None of my books would be possible without you!

Prologue

By all appearances, Hollister Cain—at sixty-seven years old and recovering from his third massive heart attack—was an inch from death, but it was an inch he clung to with the same ferocity with which he'd ruled the Cain empire for the past forty-four years.

It wasn't love that brought his entire brood rushing to his bedside. When his estranged wife, three sons—two legitimate, one bastard—and, yes, even his former daughter-in-law dropped everything at his beck and call, it was not out of devotion but rather sheer disbelief that the man who had launched a financial empire and sculpted their own lives might turn out to be a mere mortal like the rest of them.

Six weeks before, when his health had taken such a drastic turn for the worse, the first-floor study of his house in the prestigious River Oaks neighborhood of Houston had been converted into a state-of-the-art hospital room. Hollister's ornately carved mahogany desk had been removed, along with the leather wingback chairs and the Edwardian demilune bar.

Undaunted by three heart attacks, double bypass surgery and a failing liver, he still felt a long-term stay in the hospital was beneath him. The arrogant fool.

Though Dalton let himself into the room as silently as he could, Hollister's eyes flickered open. He released a slow, rasping breath. "You're late."

"Of course I am. I was at a board meeting."

His father would have known this since Cain Enterprises' board of directors had met every Monday morning at eight for over twenty years. Sometimes it seemed Hollister delighted in forcing Dalton to choose between familial obligations and the company, as if Dalton needed reminding that running Cain Enterprises was a life-consuming endeavor.

Hollister gave a slight but satisfied nod, confirming what Dalton's gut had already told him. His father was still testing him to make sure his first and only loyalty lay with the company.

"Very well." Hollister reached for the bed's controller with a frail, trembling hand. He seemed barely strong enough to press the button to raise the head of the bed.

The bed itself moved slowly, as if echoing Hollister's strain, and in the moments it took for Hollister to adjust it, Dalton scanned the room again. His mother sat on the chair immediately at his father's side, her posture stiff, even for her. Griffin Cain, Dalton's youngest brother, stood just behind their mother, looking understandably tired since he's just flown in from Scotland the day before. On Hollister's other side stood Portia, Dalton's ex-wife, seemingly more at home within the family than Dalton himself had ever felt. Portia was one of the few people both Hollister and Caro liked, which was why she was still a fixture in their lives so long after the divorce. And finally, off in the corner, gazing out the window, as far removed as ever, was Cooper Larsen, Hollister's illegitimate son.

Cooper did not even glance in Dalton's direction—or Hollister's for that matter—but rather lounged negligently against the window's frame, his expression bored, his attention elsewhere. Cooper's disinterest didn't surprise Dalton nearly as much as his actual presence did. Cooper had drifted around the edges of their family for years. For Hollister to have summoned him—and for him to have actually answered the call—the situation must be dire indeed.

By the time the head of the bed was raised, the heart monitor on the medical cart was beeping in a quick rhythm, as if the effort had strained Hollister, but the man's gaze remained steady and unwavering. He reached for something on the table beside his bed. Caro Cain snapped to attention and offered up the insulated mug of ice water, carefully positioning the straw toward her husband's mouth, but Hollister swatted it away impatiently. Instead, he grabbed the item that had been resting behind the water, an innocuous white envelope. His fingers fumbled for a minute, as if he might withdraw the contents himself. When they proved too unsteady, he thrust it toward his wife.

"Read it," he barked, the order no less direct for the frailty of his voice.

Caro frowned as if momentarily confused by this turn of events, but then she pulled out the contents of the envelope and unfolded a single typed page. The paper was thin enough that Dalton could see the shadow of the printed words through the back of it.

Caro glanced once at her husband, who was lying back, eyes closed, hands folded over his broad chest. Then she read aloud. "'Dear Hollister, it has come to my attention that you are ill and that it is unlikely you will recover from the deadly turn your health has taken. So at last, the devil will take back his minion here on earth. Before you criticize my choice of words, let me assure you of the tremendous restraint I have shown in not calling you the very devil himself. You see, I am no longer the ignorant twit you once accused me of being.'"

Caro paused, looking up from the letter, confusion obvious on her face. "Is this some sort of joke?" she asked.

Hollister grunted and waved his hand in a *keep going* gesture.

"'Perhaps you do not even remember uttering those words, but, again, I assure you, I have never forgotten them. Not for one moment. You said them mere moments after having left my—'"

Caro's voice broke, and she let the letter drop into her lap.

Griffin edged closer to their mother. "This is ridiculous. Why have you called us here? Just to humiliate Mother publicly?"

"Keep reading," Hollister commanded without opening his eyes.

"I'll read it." Griffin reached for the letter.

"No!" barked Hollister. "Caro."

Caro glanced first at Griffin and then at Dalton before picking the letter up again. Griffin gave her shoulder a little squeeze.

"'Your words were spoken with such thoughtless cruelty, and for years I prayed for the opportunity to wound you as deeply as you have wounded me. And now, finally after all these years, I have found it.

"'I know how closely you guard your little empire. How you like to control everyone under your domain. How you manipulate—'" her voice broke on the word and she had to swallow before continuing "'—and control all those within your fami—'"

Dalton had had enough. He strode forward and snatched the letter out of his mother's hands. Perhaps Hollister didn't realize the strain he was placing on his wife by forcing her to read the letter aloud, but more likely, he just didn't care.

Dalton scanned the letter and then tossed it down onto the bed so that it landed on his father's chest. He dropped it by instinct, so strong was the hatred and venom in the letter. He was almost surprised that the thing didn't burst into flames and burn a hole clear through Hollister. It had obviously been crafted to wound him. Since it hadn't killed him yet, Dalton summed up the contents of the letter for the others, though he assumed they would eventually all read it themselves.

"She claims to have given birth to a daughter of Hollister's—the missing heiress, she calls her. She refuses to tell Hollister anything other than that. She intends for it to be a form of torture for Hollister, going to his deathbed, knowing that he will never find this daughter of his."

Dalton looked first at his mother and then at Griffin. Griffin's hand had tightened on their mother's shoulder, and she seemed to be summoning the kind of strength that had served her so well through the many years of her marriage. Of course they all knew about Hollister's philandering: Cooper was living proof of it.

Cooper pushed himself away from the window frame, speaking without even glancing in Hollister's direction. "So the old man has even more bastard children. I hardly see what that has to do with us."

Personally, Dalton was inclined to agree. Didn't he have enough on his plate running Cain Enterprises?

Before anyone else could comment, Hollister opened his eyes again. "I want you to find her."

"You want *me* to find her?" Cooper asked.

"All of you," Hollister wheezed. "Any of you."

Perfect. This was exactly what Dalton needed: more responsibility. "I'm sure we can find a private investigator who specializes in this sort of thing."

"No P.I.s," Hollister barked. "Against the rules."

"Rules?" Griffin asked. "You want us to find her. Fine. We'll find her. But this isn't some sort of game."

Hollister's cracked lips twisted into a humorless smile. "Not a game. A test."

Cooper let out a bark of bitter laughter. "Of course it is. Why else would you have asked me to come if it didn't involve me having to somehow prove that I was worthy of being your son?"

"Don't be ridic—" Hollister broke off as a series of body-wrenching coughs seized him "—ridiculous. The test is—" more coughing "—for all of you."

"Regardless of the rules, I have better things to do with my time than to jump through your hoops," Griffin said. "So you can count me out. I'm not interested."

"Me neither," said Cooper.

"You will be."

Hollister said it with such absolute conviction a chill went through Dalton. Their father may be weak—he may even be dying—but Dalton had learned long ago that Hollister never spoke with conviction unless he knew he could back it up.

As if he'd read Dalton's thoughts, Hollister turned his rheumy blue gaze to Dalton. "You will all be interested, because whichever one of you finds this missing heiress will inherit all of Cain Enterprises."

Well, that certainly changed things.

Dalton had always known his father was a jerk, but this? He'd never imagined his father was capable of this.

Dalton had devoted his life to Cain Enterprises. He wasn't going to give it up without a fight. "And what happens if no one finds her?" he found himself asking.

A hush seemed to fall over the room as Hollister sucked in one rattling breath after another before finally whispering, "My entire fortune will revert to the state."

One

"He's not really going to do it," Griffin said, as he unlocked the door to his condo and stepped aside to let Dalton in. "Cain Enterprises means as much to him as it does to any of us. He'd never let the state sell off his share of the company."

"If it was any other man, I'd agree." Dalton waited until Griffin had flipped on the lights before walking into the living room. "But he doesn't bluff. You know that."

Griffin owned the penthouse condo of the downtown highrise where Dalton also lived. When Portia had asked for a divorce, Dalton had purchased the condo two floors down from Griffin's. The building was close to work but overpriced. Its main appeal was that because he'd been to Griffin's condo, he could buy it without having to waste a day following around some Realtor.

Griffin's condo was decorated in sleek cream leather and a lot of chrome. It was expensive and modern and, Dalton also thought, overly stark. On the other hand, his own condo was still decorated in mid-century-kicked-out-of-my-house-style, so he had little room to criticize.

Dalton headed straight for the sectional that dominated the space in front of the TV. Griffin gestured toward the wet bar tucked into the corner. He nodded to the row of bottles. "What'll you have?"

Dalton glanced at his watch. "It's not even noon."

"Right. After Dad's little bombshell, I think a drink is called for."

"Fine." Who was he to argue a point like that? And maybe a stiff drink would steady the rug that felt like it had been jerked out from under his feet. "I'll have a scotch."

Griffin rolled his eyes as if to say he thought Dalton was an idiot. Then he pulled out several bottles—none of which contained scotch—and started pouring splashes into a cocktail shaker.

"Do you have any idea if he can legally do this?"

"Unfortunately, I think he can." Dalton ran a hand through his hair. "Of course, Mother will still get all of their co-mingled assets—the houses, cars and their money. But all of his Cain stock is his to do with as he pleases. It would have been split evenly between the three of us. Now, who knows what will happen."

"I figure you have the most to lose here. What are you going to do?"

Dalton slipped out of his jacket and draped it over the arm of the sofa. Sighing, he sat down and scrubbed a hand down his face. When it came to this crazy scheme of his father's, he undoubtedly had the most to lose. He'd devoted his entire life to becoming the perfect future CEO of Cain Enterprises. Every choice he'd made from the time he was ten—from his hobbies as a child to his extracurricular activities in high school, to his college education, to the woman he married—had been about Cain Enterprises. He wasn't going to let his father piss it all away on a whim.

"One option is to wait until the bastard actually dies and then take the matter to court."

Griffin popped the top on the silver shaker and then gave it a vigorous jiggle. "At which point, all Father's assets will be tied up in litigation for a decade or so. Good plan."

Dalton leaned forward, propping his elbows on his knees. "If he wasn't already on his deathbed, I'd kill him for this."

"I'd help." Griffin chuckled as he scooped ice into glasses and then covered the ice with whatever concoction he'd mixed up. "On the bright side, the board loves you. Even if Father's assets did revert to the state, all his Cain stock would be sold, right? He alone doesn't even have a controlling majority. The board would most likely keep you on."

"And then you could keep your job as VP of international relations as well."

Griffin gave a little chuckle. "Yes. That would be ideal."

They both knew Griffin's job was a cushy one and not the kind he was likely to find anywhere else.

Griffin sliced a lime into wedges, squeezed one into each glass and then tossed another on top. "Sure, you'd be less insanely rich, but you'd still be CEO of Cain Enterprises."

"That would be the best-case scenario, yes." Dalton took the glass his brother handed him and eyed the pale green concoction. "This isn't scotch."

"Two years as a mixologist in college. I think I can do better than pouring you a scotch. This is me broadening your horizons."

Dalton took a hesitant sip. It was surprisingly good, less sweet than a margarita and with enough punch to knock a grown man on his ass—especially one who'd already been knocked on his ass once that day.

"Yes, the board might keep me on." In his experience, best-case scenarios were little more than daydreams. Reality was rarely so convenient. "It's far more likely that one of our competitors would snatch up all that Cain stock and make a bid to take over the company. Sheppard Capital is ideally positioned right now to do just that. In which case, I would most likely be fired and Cain Enterprises would be dismantled bit by bit."

For once, Griffin's characteristic charming grin was pressed into a grim line. He raised his glass and said bitterly, "To our loving father."

Dalton tapped his brother's glass and then downed a sizable gulp, almost hoping that this drink would do him in. He and Griffin had never been particularly close. Hollister had fostered too much rivalry between them for that. Even now, though they were united in their mutual disgust for their father's stunt, he had still pitted them against each other.

With the heat of the liquor still burning down his throat, Dalton voiced the question he had to ask: "Are you going to try to find her?"

Griffin made a face like he was about to spew cocktail across the room. "God, no. What would I want with Cain Enterprises?"

"Just had to check." Another thought occurred to Dalton. "There's one possibility we haven't considered. Cooper could find the girl."

Cooper was definitely a wild card in the equation. Dalton and Griffin had been seven and four, respectively, when Hollister brought home the then five-year-old Cooper and introduced him as his other son. He spent summers with them until Cooper's mother passed away when Cooper was sixteen. Cooper had lived with them for nearly two years, raising as much hell as he could, before going away to college. They hadn't exactly bonded.

Griffin tossed back the last of his drink. "Cooper could dismantle the company just as easily as Grant Sheppard could."

True enough… Dalton stared at the murky green dregs of his drink. If Cooper found the heiress, Cain Enterprises wouldn't be Dalton's—not the way it was meant to be.

Griffin dribbled the last bit of the drink from the cocktail shaker into both of their glasses. "So how are you going to find this mysterious sister of ours?"

"That's the question of the day, isn't it?" Hollister had been a philandering jerk for his entire married life. "It's not an issue of finding the mother so much as it is narrowing down the possibilities."

Griffin gave a bark of laughter. "Who did he meet that he didn't sleep with?"

"Exactly. When we look at it from this direction, the list of potential mothers has to be—" Dalton just shook his head, not even wanting to imagine how many women his father could have slept with. Hollister had had at least one long-term mistress when Dalton was a child, but he was afraid Sharlene was just the tip of the iceberg.

Griffin must have remembered as well. "She could be from anywhere. Any woman, in any bar, in any state in the country."

"Or from any number of foreign countries as well."

Cooper had been raised in Vale, but when Dalton had done the math—which he'd been very curious about at seven—he'd figured his father hadn't been anywhere near Colorado at the right time. However, he had been skiing in Switzerland. Since Cooper's mother had been an Olympic-caliber skier, Dalton figured they must have met there.

Thinking aloud, Dalton said, "It would be impossible to track down every woman he might have slept with during the right time, even if we could narrow down the time frame."

"Did you happen to notice the postmark on the letter?" Griffin asked.

"Yes. No return address, postmarked from the local mail station. Which is pretty smart, if she doesn't want to be found. Maybe it means she lives right around the corner. Maybe it means she lives in Toronto and paid someone to mail the letter for her."

Dalton swirled the last of the drink around the bowl of the glass as he considered their predicament. "No, the question isn't who did he sleep with. The question is, which one of those women hated him enough afterward to do something like this?"

Griffin pretended to consider, then shrugged as if giving up. "I'd guess all of them."

But Dalton shook his head. "No. Say what you will about him, but our father was a charming bastard. So that eliminates all the one-night stands and casual hookups. Someone had to really know him to hate him this much."

Dalton stood and picked up his suit coat.

Griffin raised his eyebrows. "I take it you've had an inspiration."

"Of a sort. If there's someone who hates Father that much, there's one woman who would know about it. Mrs. Fortino."

"Our former housekeeper?"

"Exactly. She knew everything that went on in that house. She'll be able to tell me what I need to know."

"She retired five years ago," Griffin pointed out. "Are you sure you can find her? Maybe she's traveling the country in a mobile home."

"She's not the one I'm worried about finding." Dalton tossed back the last of his drink. "She's not the type to travel, and she was set in her ways even when we were kids. I'm sure she's still in Houston."

"Hey, you know who would know how to find her?" Griffin asked just before Dalton walked out the door.

"Our mother," Dalton stated the obvious.

"Sure, maybe. But I was thinking of Laney."

Dalton turned and looked at his younger brother, keeping his expression carefully blank, hiding the way his heart had leaped at the sound of her name.

"You remember Laney. Mrs. Fortino's granddaughter. Lived with her for a while when we were in high school."

"Yeah. I remember her."

"She moved back to town a couple of years ago. I ran into her at a fundraiser for Tisdale. Did you know she teaches there now?"

"No, I didn't."

"Yeah. Weird, huh? I can't imagine a firecracker like Laney teaching first grade at a Catholic school."

"Guess things have changed."

Again he tried to leave, but before he made it out the door, Griffin said, "I'm surprised you didn't know she taught there. Aren't you on their board?"

"Sure, but it's a position in name only since we donate so much to the school." Dalton pulled his phone out of his pocket and glanced down at it, as if he'd just gotten a text. Then he gave the phone a little waggle to indicate he needed to go handle something. "I'll see you later?"

This time, he didn't give Griffin a chance to answer but beat a hasty retreat to the elevator.

He could have gone back in to work—he certainly had plenty to do—but instead he headed back to his condo so he could start the search for Matilda Fortino. Logic—as well as his gut—told him it was the first step in finding the missing heiress.

But for the first time in a long time—maybe in his life—he was questioning both. Was he seeking out Mrs. Fortino because she could lead him to the missing heiress or because she could lead him to Laney?

Of course, he knew where Laney was; at least, he knew where she worked. He hadn't yet gone so far as to hunt down her home address. That alone said volumes.

It said almost as much about him as the lie he'd told to Griffin. Not only had he known when Laney applied at Tisdale but he'd been the one to step in and make sure she got the job. At the time, he'd told himself it was just because she was an old family friend. Of course, at the time he'd been married to Portia. Any fantasies he'd had about Laney had been distant blips from his youth.

But now, nearly a year out from his divorce, with his entire future on the line, he had to wonder. He wasn't used to questioning his gut. But he also wasn't used to lying. So which was it: Was he looking for the missing heiress or for Laney?

* * *

At 3:00 p.m., Laney Fortino stood in front of Tisdale Elementary School cursing the hot sun, the parents who were late for pick up, Dalton Cain and the lack of specificity of fortune cookies.

Her fortune with last night's takeout had read: "Change is in your future."

Then today, she'd gotten a note from the school secretary saying Dalton Cain was coming by to talk to her after school.

It was the first accurate fortune she'd gotten in her entire life, and it had done her absolutely no good. Why couldn't it have said, "Dalton Cain is going to call" or even "Change is in your future, so tomorrow would be a great day to wear some kick-ass heels and that Betsey Johnson dress you bought on eBay. And your Spanx."

Of course, she would never wear Spanx or heels to teach in—too much bending—and if the fortune had referenced Cain directly, she probably would have booked a flight to… oh, say, Tahiti, and been halfway around the world by now.

So instead, here she was, waiting for the last of the parents to pick up their kids, sweating in the blazing October sun in her vintage sundress she'd picked up at the thrift store and her bobby socks and Keds shoes. She was dressed like a Cabbage Patch Kid.

She didn't actually care how she was dressed for Dalton Cain. It was just costuming, really. She might not care about how she looked, but she cared desperately what he *thought* about how she looked. She needed to make the right first impression.

Because there was only one reason why one of the richest, most powerful men in Houston was coming to see her. He must know her grandmother had stolen nearly a million dollars from the Cains.

Money that Laney hadn't known anything about before she'd been granted power of attorney the year before.

Ever since discovering the extra funds in Gran's trust,

Laney had been racked with guilt wondering what to do about it. There was no way Gran had come by the money honestly. Laney knew roughly how much Gran had had when Laney had graduated from high school. No amount of frugality or clever investing could turn her meager savings into well over a million dollars in a decade.

Gran must have stolen the money from the Cains.

Laney couldn't very well go to the authorities. It seemed unlikely they'd prosecute an elderly woman with Alzheimer's, but what if they did? Laney couldn't risk it. She certainly couldn't go to the Cains and explain. Hollister was brutal and vindictive to his enemies and Caro was little better. Every time Laney tried to think of a way out of the conundrum, she pictured Gran being led away to jail in handcuffs.

She couldn't even just give the money back. It was in an irrevocable trust, which Gran had set up to pay for her care at the assisted-living center. Laney couldn't touch it. Her power of attorney extended only so far. So there she was trapped with the knowledge of a wrong she had no way to right. And terrified that Dalton Cain had somehow discovered the truth.

Either he was going to prosecute her defenseless eighty-three-year-old grandmother or he was going to make her return the money.

Neither option was acceptable, which meant Laney had to consider very carefully how she wanted to play this.

Her default reaction to any of the Cains—especially Dalton—was bravado and indignation. Ten years ago—when she'd last seen Dalton—she'd been a completely different person. That girl would have dressed up in her most provocative outfit, dared him to call the police and then hurled insults and cuss words at him as they hauled her off to jail. But she wasn't that brash, rebellious girl anymore.

The previous decade had taught her moderation and restraint. She was an elementary-school teacher, for goodness' sake. So maybe it wasn't a bad thing she looked like a Cabbage Patch Kid, all soft, cuddly and compliant.

No sooner had the thought passed through her head than a sleek cream sedan turned the corner onto Beacon Street and headed for the school. She couldn't say how she knew, but she knew instantly that Dalton was driving that car. Maybe it was because she was familiar with most of the cars the parents drove. Or maybe it was the way the car practically oozed down the road.

The cream car slid into one of the visitor parking spots, and sure enough, out climbed Dalton. She recognized him instantly, even though the last time she'd seen him had been more than a decade ago when she'd moved out of her grandmother's apartment right after she turned eighteen. Today he was dressed in tan slacks and a white oxford shirt. He paused and slipped his sunglasses down to look at her over their top, as if not quite sure he recognized her. She gave a little half wave, and then he walked toward her.

Beside her, Ellie—the last of her car-pool kids—squirmed. "Ms. Fortino, you're hurting my hand."

"Huh?" Laney glanced down. "Oh, sorry." She loosened her grip then gave Ellie's hand a little rub.

Ellie frowned as she nodded suspiciously toward the parking lot. "Who's that strange man over there? He's been waving at you. We should go tell Principal Shippey."

"No!" Jeez, that was just what she needed. Ellie's mom's Buick finally—finally!—pulled to a stop in front of the school. "He's an...old friend of mine."

Liar, liar, pants on fire.

"Next time, karma, okay?" she muttered as she handed Ellie into her mom's car. Just once, she'd like to meet Dalton Cain on even footing. But instead, she was meeting him in ruffled bobby-socks footing.

Stupid, comfortable Keds shoes.

Even though he hadn't seen her in years, Dalton instantly recognized Laney Fortino. There was no mistaking the ink-black hair that tumbled around her shoulders. She still moved with the sort of slinky sensuality that should have been at odds with her schoolteacher clothing but somehow wasn't. She had the same alabaster skin and same wide, smiling mouth.

She was dressed in a floral sundress that hit her midcalf and fluttered as she moved. A small girl stood by her side, her hand wrapped in Laney's. The girl chattered, pointing down the street at a car pulling slowly to the curb. Though a few kids were still loitering at the edges of school property, most of the students seemed to have cleared out.

For a second, the sight of her standing there stopped him dead in his tracks. A jolt of pure desire shot through him. Laney had been one of those girls who had skipped over the awkwardness of adolescence and gone straight from girl to sex goddess—a role she'd reveled in because it irritated her strict grandmother and her benefactors, his parents. It had irritated him as well, though he'd tried not to let it show. Now, womanhood had softened the raw edges of her sexuality. Her sensuality was more subtle but more attractive as well.

Before now, he questioned whether he'd done her any favors when he'd helped her get this job three years ago. He wondered if she could temper her rebellious nature enough to teach first grade—in a wealthy, conservative private school, no less. The Laney he'd known as a teenager had scorned the wealthy and despised their hypocrisies. Now she was teaching their kids.

Watching her today, he'd have never guessed that flowing dress camouflaged her defiant nature—until she bent to speak to the little girl by her side. Then, the strap of her sundress slipped to reveal the swirling line of a tattoo on her shoulder. That was more like it.

She looked at him, the full lines of her mouth flattened into disapproval. Well, one thing hadn't changed. She still hated him. He couldn't really blame her after the way he'd treated her.

Laney said something to the girl, giving her hand a pat. There was something intrinsically feminine and graceful about her appearance but certainly nothing refined or elegant. For some reason, he thought of his ex-wife then. Portia wouldn't be caught dead in a fluttery floral sundress and... were those sneakers Laney had on? He'd been married to Portia for eight years, and he wasn't even sure she had sneakers. For that matter, Portia wouldn't be caught dead standing outside a school, holding a child's hand.

Only after Laney had helped the little girl into the Buick and turned to face him with a sort of stalwart determination did he wonder why he was even thinking about Portia and Laney in the same thought. The two women were nothing alike. He'd been intimately and emotionally involved with Portia, but with Laney... He hardly knew how to describe his relationship with her. Not for the first time, he wondered exactly what he was doing here.

As Dalton stepped up onto the sidewalk, he pulled his glasses off and slid them into his shirt pocket. "Hello, Laney."

"Um. Hi. Dalton." Her words came out choked and awkward, as though she'd forgotten how to talk altogether. Jeez, between the sneakers and being suddenly struck nearly mute, this was so not her day.

She knew it was nerves—and fear—that had tied her tongue into knots. It had nothing to do with the fact that Dalton had grown into a man of such arresting attractiveness that she could hardly pull air into her lungs when he looked at her.

"Is there somewhere we can go to talk?" he asked, nodding toward the building.

"Yes. My classroom." But instead of walking inside, Laney found herself just standing there, trying not to stare at Dalton. His face was still lean, his lips still full. His dark hair still curled slightly, as if in rebellion against the relentless structure he imposed on his life.

Then, unexpectedly, she found herself looking into his eyes, as if he'd been studying her in return. Heat flooded her cheeks, and she jerked her eyes away from his.

He kept his gaze on her. She could practically feel it. "You look good, Laney."

Liar, liar, pants on fire.

She did not look good—not standing here in her thrift-store dress and her bobby socks, at the end of a long day of working with children. She'd once come home to find a Cheeto stuck in her hair. So she knew for a fact that she did not look good—at least not the way he looked good.

However, his relaxed greeting calmed her. Maybe he didn't know about the money. If he did, wouldn't he have started with that? But if he wasn't here about the money, then why was he here?

Flustered, she turned and headed for the building. "I should warn you that I can't talk long. I teach an afterschool theater class."

At the door, Laney paused before swiping her card past the electronic lock, only to find Dalton right behind her. She jerked back a step, and he reached out a hand to steady her.

She looked up from his hand to his face. He was standing closer than before, and she sucked in a sharp breath. How had she forgotten how blue his eyes were? They were such an unusual shade of blue too. The color of the sky—not the rich, deep sky-blue you saw when you looked straight up but the muted, almost sea-blue of the sky at the distant horizon. *Cain blue,* Gran had always called it.

Dalton Cain—with his *Cain blue* eyes. She couldn't let herself forget, even for a moment, who this man was—or that he had the power to crush her and Gran, if he ever had reason to do so.

Jerking her arm away from him, she asked, "What is it you want from me?"

"Why do you assume I want something from you?" he asked, his tone all innocence.

"Because when a Cain comes to visit, they always want something."

"You don't have a very high opinion of us."

"No. I don't suppose I do."

And she knew it was ironic that she didn't trust him. Of the two of them, she was the one who was aiding and abetting a thief. But what was she supposed to do? Let him cart Gran off to prison?

And suddenly, with that simple reminder, she didn't want to let him into the school with her. She wanted to do this quick and dirty, to find out what he wanted from her and get out fast. She crossed her arms over her chest, tucking the key card under one arm in an act of silly defiance. "Don't forget, I grew up in the Cain household. I would describe my opinion as accurate rather than low."

She instantly regretted her words. This was so not the dialogue of the demure damsel in distress.

But then he winced with such exaggerated pain. "Ouch."

She very nearly smiled, but she stopped herself just in time. She would not let herself be charmed by him. She knew all too well that Dalton could act like her best friend in the world one minute and not even know her the next. There was no way she would let herself get sucked into his mind games again.

"Oh, don't pretend to be wounded," she grumbled. "I haven't spoken to you in nearly a decade. If you've shown up in my life after all this time it's because you want something," she said honestly. "So why don't you stop trying to charm it out of me and just tell me what it is?"

The corner of his mouth bumped up. "You find me charming?"

She rolled her eyes. "I think we both know you can be very charming when there's enough at stake. After all, you are your father's son."

His smiled faded, along with the spark in his eyes. "Okay. You want to know why I'm here? I need to talk to your grandmother."

Damn. All the electric awareness vanished as quickly as though a circuit breaker had been blown. If he wanted to talk to Gran, then he must know.

Maybe he didn't have proof. Maybe that was why he wanted to talk to Gran. Maybe he intended to badger the truth out of her. Laney couldn't let that happen.

On a good day, Matilda Fortino barely knew who she was. As for the bad days…well, those were the days she spent trapped in her own mind, trapped in the memories of the distant past, filled with recriminations and regrets.

If Dalton went to see her, who knew what might come pouring out? She might confess to everything, assuming he didn't already have proof.

Suddenly Laney—who'd never backed down from a fight in her life—felt like running. She waved her key card across the pad and the door into the school beeped. Just as she reached to open it, Dalton placed a hand on her arm. "Will you bring me to see your grandmother?"

Laney gave Dalton what she hoped would be one final look. She slipped back into the cool sanctuary of the school as she answered, "No."

Two

Dalton shoved his foot between the door and the jamb seconds before it closed and locked him out.

Laney had her hand on the inside brass handle, and he felt her give it a tug before she glanced down to see his black leather shoe wedged there.

"Just hear me out."

Time seemed to stretch as he waited for her response. She wasn't going to listen to him. She'd slam the door in his face, he was sure of it. After all, they both knew she was right to be wary of him. Despite the difference in their ages, they'd been friends when she'd first moved into the Cain household when she was eleven. For two years, she'd shadowed him like an eager puppy. Then, abruptly and without explanation, he'd cut her out of his life the summer before her freshman year. He'd given her plenty of reasons to hate him now.

Her gaze darted all around the empty school hall before returning reluctantly to his. He saw her jaw clench and her mouth pinch in annoyance before he felt the pressure on his foot let up.

"Fine."

"Thank you." He opened the door the rest of the way and stepped out of the mid-afternoon sun into dimly lit air-conditioning. This was obviously a side entrance, leading into a broad hall with classroom doors branching out on either side. The walls were covered in murals painted by clumsy childish hands. The few blank stretches of wall were plastered with the kids' art "framed" by construction paper. Despite the obvious attempts to brighten the atmosphere, the building showed its age.

Laney all but trotted down the hall, passed the occasional open doorway. "My classroom is over here."

She moved with a speed and efficiency that belied her frilly dress and perky ruffled socks. All traces of the warmth she'd shown to the little girl in the car line had vanished.

Dalton considered himself something of an expert on reading business opponents. He was a master at the subtle art of analyzing someone's mood and temperament based on their body language and facial expressions. It was a skill that came from many years of studying people.

He needed none of those skills to read Laney today. His presence here had her freaked out. Something he'd said or done had spooked her. But what?

By the time he caught up with her, she was pushing open the door to one of the classrooms. Like the rest of the building, the room was neat and well maintained but obviously showing its age. It had been years since Dalton had been in an elementary school—twenty-one years, to be exact, since his own stint as an elementary student. He'd forgotten how undersized that world felt. The tables barely reached his knees. The chairs looked sized for dolls rather than people. There were bookcases in one corner with a cluster of beanbag chairs. Caddies of art supplies sat at each trio of desks. One adult-sized desk sat in the corner.

Laney turned when she reached that desk. An owl stuffed animal sat beside the computer monitor. She ran her fingers across the toy's white fluff, then blew out a breath before turning back to him.

"The afterschool class I teach has an assistant that oversees snack time. But I'll need to be there when the class starts in fifteen minutes, so you'd better tell me why you're really here."

Her tone was terse, and she looked as though she could barely squeeze the words out through her clenched jaw. Again, he wondered what had her so freaked out. He didn't remember Laney being a naturally nervous person: feisty, yes, jittery, no.

"My father is ill," he began.

"I'm sorry to hear that," she said, but he could tell the condolences were by rote.

"You don't have to do that."

Her brow furrowed. "What?"

"Pretend to be sorry that his health is declining." His words came out stiffer than he meant them to be. He was trying to let her off the hook, to create a common ground between them. She may not have as many reasons to hate his father as he did, but she surely had plenty.

Instead, his words ended up sounding slightly accusatory—and cold...something his father would have said. Why was it that he could talk to almost anyone except Laney?

"I..." Her frown deepened as her mouth pressed into a line of confusion. "I'm sorry. I meant no disrespect."

Shoot. He was making this even worse than it was. "I know." Why did it feel like there were many things he wanted to say to her and none of them were the right ones?

Instead of fumbling through any more explanations, he pulled out a copy of the letter and handed it to her. "A week ago my father received this."

Laney looked from him to the paper he held out. "What does it have to do with my grandmother?"

Was it his imagination, or did her voice tremble slightly? "Please read the letter. Then I'll explain."

She nodded. Her frown only deepened as she read. She glanced up after a few seconds. She must have been disconcerted at how closely he was watching her, because she turned away to finish the letter, her hand fluttering nervously by her hair as she read.

She was a quick reader, and soon she looked back at him and said, "I'm sorry, but I still don't see what this has to do with Gran."

"Hollister Cain wants this girl found."

Laney extended the letter back to him with a sigh that sounded almost relieved. "And the girl's mother seems rather determined to keep her hidden," she pointed out with an arched little smile.

Dalton found himself smiling back, despite the bizarre circumstances. "Yes, but this is Hollister we're talking about. Little things like other people's wishes don't bother him much."

"Hold on a second," Laney said abruptly. "You don't think …" She physically recoiled. "You don't think my mother wrote the letter? You don't think I'm the missing heiress?"

The expression of disgust on her face was so strong he nearly laughed. "No, of course not. Anyone who's seen a picture of your father couldn't mistake you for anyone's daughter but his."

She chuckled—and again he wondered at the relief he heard in the sound. Then she gestured to her nose. "Right. The Fortino nose. It is hard to miss."

Her nose was distinctive—a little larger than most women probably preferred and with a patrician bump—but it fit her face, blending seamlessly with the rest of her features. He'd grown up in a world where a woman's facial imperfections were stamped out like cockroaches. He loved that she'd never had her nose done, which wasn't exactly the smooth segue that would lead them back to the questions he needed answers to. So he went for direct instead.

"No, it never occurred to me that your mother might have

written the letter. But your grandmother was the Cain house-keeper for nearly thirty years. I thought she might know some-thing."

"About your father's romantic indiscretions? I can't imagine why she would. That hardly fell under her purview."

"No. She wouldn't have time to manage the house if it had." He quickly explained his reasoning. "She worked for my father longer than most Cain Enterprises employees. If my father had any secrets, she knew them. If my parents fought, she overheard it. If there's anyone with dirt on my family, it's your grandmother."

As he spoke, Laney looked down at the owl again. She ran her hand over the pretend feathers and gave the wing a little tug.

When she didn't meet his gaze, he continued, "I visited the assisted-living center she's at. They wouldn't even let me in without your approval. I need to talk to her. You have to let me see her."

Laney's shoulders stiffened. "I no longer have any connec-tion to your family. I don't *have* to do anything."

It was his turn to clench his jaw. He wasn't Hollister's son for nothing. He knew when to grovel. "Will you please grant me access to your grandmother?"

"No." She held up a hand, warding off the arguments she could see percolating. "She doesn't know anything. She can't give you any information."

Finally, she turned and met his gaze. Her own was clear and determined, but he didn't let that bother him.

"I can make it worth your while," he said.

"Of course you can. You're a Cain. You Cains are experts at making lavish promises."

"I may be a Cain, but I'm not my father. I plan on keeping any promises I make."

"Kudos to you for knowing the difference between a prom-ise made and a promise kept."

"We're not all heartless bastards," he reminded her.

"That remains to be seen." She gave the owl another pat on the head and turned to face him fully. "However, it's immaterial. I'm not keeping you from Gran on a whim. She can't help you."

"Let me talk to her. Let her decide that."

"It's not that simple. Gran has Alzheimer's. Even if she did know something, she'd be unable to tell you. If she ever knew the answers to your questions, the information is locked away in her head."

Laney's words sank slowly into his brain. Their meaning was almost incomprehensible. "Alzheimer's?" he repeated stupidly.

Laney didn't meet his gaze, and he thought there might have been a sheen of tears in her eyes.

His mind flitted through his memories of Laney's grandmother, Mrs. Fortino as he'd always called her, because his own mother had always insisted on maintaining that level of formality with the staff. Matilda Fortino had been a battleship of a woman. Serious and stern, she'd been a rock in his childhood. Where his own mother had been mercurial and temperamental, Mrs. Fortino had been stalwart and consistent—a steady force in a tumultuous household.

Suddenly he felt Laney's hand on his arm. He looked up to realize she'd crossed to stand beside him. Shock had rocked him back so he leaned against the corner of one of the bookcases.

"Didn't you know?" Her words cut through the fog her news had cast over his brain.

"No."

"I'm sorry. I assumed the assisted-living center told you why she's not allowed visitors."

"They didn't. Only that you'd have to come with me if I wanted to see her."

Laney ran a hand up and down his arm. It was a gentle gesture, meant to soothe and calm. "I'm sorry," she said again.

"If I'd known that you didn't know, I wouldn't have been so harsh."

He looked from her hand to her face and found her studying his expression. Her unusual amber eyes were wide, concern crinkled her brow. She stood close enough that the front of her dress brushed against his legs and her breasts were mere inches from his arm. He sucked in a deep breath.

This wasn't why he was here—no matter how tempting Laney Fortino was.

But all the deep-breathing exercises in the world wouldn't help—not when the scent of her filled his lungs with every inhalation. She smelled like crayons and Elmer's Glue. The unique combination should have been unappealing but wasn't. And underneath that was the smell of her soap or maybe her shampoo—something fruity and simple, clean and uncomplicated.

He nearly laughed at the thought. Laney may *smell* uncomplicated, but there was nothing uncomplicated about the way she made him feel.

He straightened away from the bookcase, which only brought her closer. She snatched her hand back as if she'd been burned and skittered away from him, retreating to the desk.

"Strangers upset her. Gran, I mean. Of course, you're not a stranger. But that's why the assisted-living center doesn't let people visit her. Her doctor thinks it's for the best."

He felt himself crumbling under the weight of her words. When he forced his gaze back to hers, it was to see her watching him with an emotion he rarely saw directed at him—an emotion he never thought he'd see in her eyes...certainly not after he'd spent so much of their teenage years treating her with disdain and scorn.

He'd known from the time he was thirteen that Laney Fortino could be his downfall. He'd known she alone had the power to bring him to his knees. He'd fought against it with every tool in his juvenile arsenal. He'd been rude, condescending and—occasionally—downright mean.

Laney had looked at him with the sting of pain, feisty rebellion and with downright anger. But until now, she'd never looked at him with sympathy.

Three

Given their troubled history, she should have enjoyed seeing defeat flicker across Dalton's face. Maybe time had mellowed out her dislike of him. Or maybe it was just that…jeez, they were talking about *Gran*. How could she be upset with anyone—even Dalton—who got this choked up about Gran?

So often she felt as though she was all alone in caring for her gran—no father, no siblings. Yes, the staff at the assisted-living facility took care of her grandmother, but they didn't care about her. And they didn't offer Laney the emotional support a loved one would. So maybe it was natural that she went all gooey inside when she saw Dalton openly devastated by the news.

"I'm so sorry, Dalton. I had no idea Gran meant so much to you."

He glanced up, surprise flickering across his features.

Instantly, she knew she'd guessed wrong. She blew out a huff of annoyance as she walked over to the nearest cluster of tables and began picking stray crayons off the floor. "Never mind."

He watched her for a moment in silence, then said, "You're annoyed with me."

She set aside a picture book with a sigh. "No. I'm annoyed with myself. For a minute there, I actually felt sorry for you. I forgot you're a Cain. Heartless and cold, just like the rest of them."

She frowned at her own words. She was heartless and cold—glacial, practically. Except for the moment when she'd touched his arm. He'd looked up at her with genuine heat in his gaze. She'd swear it. What was she supposed to do with that?

Before she could find any answers, he spoke. "Is that really what you think of me?"

Shaking her head, she shoved a few crayons into one of the buckets before moving on to the next cluster of tables. "What else am I supposed to think? I tell you my grandmother has Alzheimer's, and you feign sympathy to manipulate me?" She looked up at him, half expecting him to dodge her gaze in shame. He didn't. "I didn't expect even you to be that much of a jerk."

"You don't think I'm sorry your grandmother has Alzheimer's? Your grandmother was really important to me."

She snorted, snaking her foot under a desk to nudge a marker out into the open. "Don't overplay your hand. Polite condolences would be believable. But a Cain would never display actual grief over the hired help."

"You think I'm such an ass I couldn't muster any emotion for the woman who kept house for us for nearly three decades?" His tone was flat and cold.

"No. I just think you're most upset that you won't get to grill her for information."

She paused as she said the words and it hit her. He was here to grill Gran for info regarding his father. That meant he didn't know about the money. She should be relieved. She *was*. But she was also annoyed with him for trying to manipulate her.

Hoping to dislodge her contrariness, she shook her head and said, "I don't believe Gran was important to you. She was neither caring nor attentive. She didn't inspire gushing feelings of warmth and affection, even from me."

Dalton opened his mouth as if he might protest, but then he shut it again with a fair-enough shrug.

"My grandmother was efficient and competent. She ran the Cain household like it was inside of a Swiss pocket watch. But she was not the kind of woman people love. People tolerate her, mostly because they like her cooking. But they don't love her."

She straightened, crossed back to the desk and grabbed her school keys. "Now, if you'll excuse me, my afternoon class starts in five minutes."

She plucked her purse and tote bag from the corner behind her desk and marched toward the door, holding it open for Dalton with something of a dramatic flair.

She couldn't help wondering if she'd pushed too far. Dalton straightened, his expression impossible to read. His mouth was set in a humorless line, but mischief danced about his eyes.

He walked toward her slowly, without ever taking his hands from his pockets. Instead of preceding her out the door, he stopped, close enough that she inched back a step until the doorknob pressed into the small of her back.

His stance was vaguely threatening—there was something in the way he stood too close. Or maybe it was just that, for her, he was always too close. Or maybe it was the way he looked at her, his gaze steadily taking in every one of her features and imperfections.

When he spoke, it was slowly, as if each word was meant to build her dread, but foolish girl that she was, she didn't feel the threat, only the thrill.

"Laney, if you are so convinced I'm the bad guy here, then I'll play the bad guy. I'm more than happy to be the big bad wolf to your industrious little piggy."

Refusing to back down from him, she bumped up her chin. "I'm not afraid of you."

He did another one of those slow, lingering perusals of her face, and her cheeks burned under his gaze. "Maybe you should be."

Maybe he was right. Maybe she should be afraid, but she wasn't. She straightened her spine, and the action closed some of the distance between them, bringing her breasts to within a micrometer of his chest.

"Maybe," she said. "But I'm not a little girl anymore and—"

"Thank God."

She ignored his muttered interruption. "And none of the Cains have power over me anymore. I've made sure of that."

Of course, that was a bald-faced lie, because if he found out about the money, then he most certainly would have power over her—a lot of it.

She pushed past him, even though it meant brushing her chest against his, even though it made heat stir in her belly and her nipples tighten against the cloth of her bra.

She was three steps down the hall when he asked, "Just how sure about that are you?"

She kept walking.

Ten steps later he said, "How's that theater camp of yours?"

Her steps slowed, even as her heart rate picked up. He didn't know what he was talking about. He couldn't. He must just be guessing based on what she'd said earlier.

"The Fairyland Theater or something, isn't it?"

Damn it!

She stopped, pressing her eyes closed. If he'd really been guessing, he wouldn't have come so close.

She turned around to glare at him. "The Woodland Theater."

Dalton, damn him, stood right where she'd left him, hands in his pockets, smirk on his face.

It took a great deal of restraint—restraint she would not have had just a few years ago—not to stalk down the hall and slap that smile off his face. She was not a woman of violence, but it had been a trying day.

"Cut to the chase, and stop wasting my time. What exactly do you know about the Woodland Theater?"

"I know it's your pet project. It's the class you teach after school. I know you spend two hours every day after normal school hours running this enrichment program and that it's mostly underprivileged kids—some who are scholarship kids here at the school, others who are bused in from other neighborhoods. Thirty kids total. And I know the program is funded entirely by donations."

He knew more than she wished he did.

True, not all of his information was correct—it was thirty-two kids, and nearly half the kids were not, strictly speaking, "underprivileged." Though that was a term she had problems with. All of the kids in her program had a hard time of it. She wasn't sure the emotionally neglected kids from wealthy families had it any better off than the poor kids.

"I see you did your research," she said flatly. Sure, of all the secret knowledge he could have, she should probably be glad this was it. On the other hand, Woodland was *hers*. She didn't want his sticky Cain fingers anywhere near it.

Dalton's smirk twisted into a smile but not a pleasant one. "Did you really expect any less of me?"

"No." She'd just been blindsided, because he'd stuck his finger in a different pot than one she'd been expecting. "Of course I'm not surprised. This is what Cains do, isn't it? You find someone's weakness and exploit it."

For just an instant, Dalton's smile faltered. "Maybe I don't want to be that kind of Cain."

"Well, then, maybe you shouldn't be threatening my theater program."

"Maybe I'm not." He stepped away from her classroom door, letting it close behind him as he walked toward her. "I don't think the Woodland Theater program is your weakness. It seems like a great program. Exactly the kind of thing I'd expect you to be involved in."

She eyed him warily. "And..."

"And it should continue. I'm sure finding funding is difficult in this economic climate."

"So you *are* threatening me."

"Not at all. Think of it as promising. If you help me, I can make sure your afterschool program has enough funding for years."

"Aah. So you're not threatening. You're bribing."

"Exactly."

"How much money are you talking about?"

"How much do you need?"

"I'm serious, Dalton."

"So am I. You want me to fund the whole program. I'll fund it. You'll never have to write another grant proposal. You'll never have to go brownnosing for money again. All you have to do is let me talk to your grandmother."

For a long moment, Laney stood there, frozen in the hall, considering his offer. The ticking clock on the wall seemed overly loud, giving the impression that she and Dalton were all alone in the school, even though Laney knew the other teachers must still be working in their classrooms.

She didn't want to say yes. She didn't want Dalton anywhere near her grandmother. She didn't want him in her life at all. But the offer he was making her was far too tempting to walk away from.

It wasn't even that she couldn't resist the money he was offering. She could. Money was just…money. If funding got tight, she'd find a way to make it work. She always had in the past.

No, she couldn't resist the offer because he'd made it so tempting. Not many people would walk away from that kind of promise. So if she did, it would look suspicious. A Cain would never understand someone turning down money. He'd want to know why she'd done it. He'd get curious. He'd start digging. And there were secrets she didn't want him to know.

No, if he was going to be unearthing any skeletons from the past, they needed to be his father's skeletons, not her grandmother's. She needed to keep him focused on that mystery, even if it meant helping him.

"Okay." She turned and started walking again, trusting that he'd catch up with her. "Let's talk numbers."

She heard the rhythm of his steps as he jogged a few steps and then fell in line beside her. "How much does it cost a year to run this program?"

"A hundred thousand dollars." She threw out a number.

His pace faltered. "For thirty kids? You're joking."

"No. If you're paying, then I'm giving myself a raise and hiring someone else to help." This wasn't actually about the money. She just wanted a number big enough to scare him off. "Besides, this way we can double enrollment."

He placed a hand on her arm. "Hey, this isn't a golden ticket, you know."

"Are you sure? Because you sure made it sound like it was."

Despite her resolve, she could hardly keep a quiver from her voice. It might be a cliché, but she felt like she was playing with fire here. As much as she wanted to believe it was about protecting her grandmother, or even about the money, she worried that it was something more—that she was looking for his buttons to push just because it had always been so much fun to push them.

In all those years they'd lived under the same roof—Dalton the stoically perfect, obnoxious rich kid, Laney the trashy poor girl—she'd never actually gotten a rise out of him. But, dear Lord, trying to had been her favorite pastime. Why hadn't she grown out of it?

She looked down at his hand on her arm and then back up at him. She tried to forget how much fun it was to needle him, to remember the part she had to play. The Cain family had typecast her a long time ago, just as much as she had typecast them.

"Look, you need something from me, and it's not a small thing either. I'm not doing this to be greedy. I'm just trying to protect my grandmother." Well, that at least was true. "Letting you see her is going to upset her. It'll be hard, and sometimes it takes her weeks to recover from a single bad day."

She expected some kind of reaction from him there. Most people—nearly everyone—didn't like to talk about her grandmother's Alzheimer's. When the topic couldn't be avoided, usually there was a lot of awkward hemming and hawing. But Dalton just looked at her.

So she continued. "Besides, it's not like the Cains can't spare the money. Cain Enterprises is worth billions. You could probably trim this much from the corporate-office floral budget without anyone blinking an eye."

"We don't actually have a corporate floral budget."

"Don't pretend you can't afford it." By now they'd reached the doors to the cafeteria. She could hear the kids on the other side. The Tisdale kids were finishing up their afterschool snacks. The kids who were bused in from Houston Independent School District had arrived. She could hear the eager gurgle of noise bubbling out through the door. This was her real life, she reminded herself. This was where she belonged. Pushing Dalton's buttons might be fun, but her obligations lay beyond this door with the children she taught.

"Do we have a deal?"

"We do."

"A hundred thousand dollars for the chance to speak with my grandmother?"

Chagrin flickered across his face, and she could have sworn his jaw was spasming. "Yes."

"Okay, then." She turned her back on him and set off through the cafeteria doors, but he stopped her before she could disappear into her inner sanctum.

"When will you be done here? I'll send a driver to pick you up, and we can visit your grandmother tonight."

She let out a scoff of derision before she realized he was serious. "Um...no. Not a chance."

He gave her a flat look. "You just agreed."

"Yes. But I didn't just agree to give away the milk for

free." Then she waved her hand dismissively so he wouldn't think—okay, wouldn't know—that she had sex on the brain. "I agreed to help you after you've paid me that ridiculous amount of money. Not before. You want access to my grandmother, you pay up."

"You want me to just give you a hundred thousand dollars? It's not that simple."

"Of course *I* don't want the money. Don't just give it to me." She fluttered her hand around. "Do all that stuff we agreed to."

"All that stuff we agreed to? Like I should just run off and have my lawyers set up a trust for the charity you work for and drop a hundred thousand dollars into it."

"Exactly." Again, she turned to leave, trusting that this was where he'd come to his senses and walk away. Again, he stopped her.

"Come on, Laney. I don't have that kind of time. I need answers now."

"And I'm sure that with the full power of Cain Enterprises behind you, you'll make it happen quickly."

He narrowed his gaze, but he didn't contradict her. Just when she was sure he was going to tell her to forget it, he nodded.

It was bizarre, how easily she'd gotten everything she'd asked for. In the end, despite the rumble of kid voices calling to her from the cafeteria, she had one last question she couldn't let go of.

"Tell me something, Dalton. Why go to all this trouble? I know you've always been your father's go-to guy, but this is crazy. Why are you still jumping through so many hoops for him?"

"Because he still controls Cain Enterprises. If I don't find this missing heiress, I'm going to lose it all."

Four

Less than twenty-four hours later, Laney held a nearly half-inch-thick stack of papers in her hand. She ran her thumb over the edges and watched the pages flutter.

"So he really did it?" she asked. "He did everything he said he would?"

Her next-door neighbor Brandon took off his glasses and pinched the bridge of his nose. "Yes. As far as I can tell. Though, I'm no expert, mind you."

Brandon owned the duplex where she lived. The cottage, in a funky little college neighborhood, was charming, cozy and perfect for her minimalist life, since his half was bigger than hers. She'd always suspected he was gay beneath his button-down lawyer exterior, but he'd never shared so much as a millimeter of his private life with her. She didn't mind, though, since it was his prerogative. Besides, he was the kind of neighbor one could trust with spare keys, and he'd come over to kill bugs for her on more than one occasion—even big, nasty spiders. And he seemed totally willing to offer legal advice in exchange for wine, which in her mind put him up for some sort of handiest-neighbor-of-all-time award.

Laney tossed the stack of papers onto her coffee table and reached for her glass of wine. "You're a lawyer."

"An intellectual-property lawyer." Brandon leaned forward to pour more wine into his own glass.

"That's still two years of school and a bar exam closer to being an expert than I am."

"Do I think he intends to donate the money to Woodland Theater? Yes, I do."

"Oh." Laney tried to drown the sick feeling in her belly with a gulp of wine.

She hadn't really believed he would do it. She hadn't actually intended to take his money. She'd thought if she made it difficult enough for him to see Gran that he'd back off and leave them all in peace. She should have known better. Cains never backed down from a fight. They were in it until the end. She should have remembered that.

She groaned and dropped her chin into her palm. "I'm in over my head. I should have known better than to try to go up against a Cain." She looked up at Brandon. "I'm going to get crushed, aren't I?"

"You make it sound like you're facing Dalton on the field of battle."

"Well, in my experience, any dealings with the Cains are like war." Brandon gave a snort. "You wouldn't agree?"

Brandon took a long sip of his wine, rolling it on his tongue as though he was quite the connoisseur—or like he was carefully considering his next words. She'd shared enough wine with him to know he wasn't a connoisseur.

"Come on, Brandon, you know me too well to mince words. If you have an opinion, spit it out."

He swallowed. "Okay. I think you're rushing this."

"You think I'm in over my head?"

"No. It's not that. It's just—" He took another gulp of wine, and this time it went down fast. "You've got all these opinions about the Cains. Opinions that you formed when you were still a kid. And—"

"You think I don't know the Cains?"

Brandon held up a hand to stave off her annoyance. "I think you know Hollister Cain. He's exactly the conniving, backstabbing bastard you say he is."

There was a *but* dangling on the end of Brandon's sentence just as loud as a shout. "But you think I'm wrong about Dalton."

Brandon shrugged. "Ever since he took over, the company atmosphere has been different. He's still ruthless. Still aggressive as hell when it comes to business, but he's not sneaky and manipulative like his father was. Hollister Cain was the kind of guy who'd steal corporate secrets right out from under your nose and then if you tried to come after him, he'd sue you for infringement of his intellectual property. Then he'd buy off the judge to ensure he won the case. Then he'd take the money from the settlement to buy up your stock and bury your company."

"Yeah, that sounds about right." Just what Laney needed— a reminder of how ruthlessly Hollister would go after Gran if he ever found out about the money she had stolen. True, it sounded as if Hollister was on his deathbed, but she didn't believe for a minute that he would let something as trifling as his own mortality keep him from prosecuting someone who'd done him wrong.

"Dalton isn't like that."

"Well, maybe it's just harder to buy off judges now than it was thirty years ago."

"No. I don't think it's that." But Brandon still chuckled as he shook his head. "Both times I went up against him, there was no sneakiness. No manipulation. If he wants your company, you know he's coming for it. Everything out in the open. So honest and fair it's almost ridiculous. It's almost like he's trying to redeem the company's reputation."

Laney could feel herself frowning. Suddenly she was aware

of how closely Brandon was watching her. Disconcerted, she set her glass down. "So you think I'm wrong about Dalton Cain?"

"I can't guarantee that he's not trying to screw you over." Brandon pushed the document across the table toward her. "But I'd be very surprised if he was."

Laney nervously tapped her nail tip on the stem of her glass. If Brandon was to be believed, Dalton was not the corporate predator his father had been. In fact, he may actually be a decent human being.

What was she supposed to do with that?

If Dalton really was on the up-and-up, she couldn't take his money. Sure, the Cains probably donated this kind of money all the time. And, sure, the Woodland Theater was a worthy cause—the kids she worked with desperately needed the extra attention. But she'd still manipulated him into donating it and that felt wrong.

Better to know all this now than after all the papers had been signed.

She lifted her glass in silent toast to Brandon. "Thank you. And thank goodness you were willing to work for cheap wine. I could never afford to hire a lawyer."

"I'm not saying it's ironclad or anything," Brandon said hastily. "If the guy wanted to back out, I'm sure he could find a way. How much do you trust Dalton?"

She considered the question, but since she had no real answer, she was forced to hedge with an indecisive waggle of her hand. "Enough, I suppose."

"I thought this guy tormented you in high school."

Dalton had been such an arrogant ass back in school—not brash and pushy, the way jocks always were, but just ice-cold and dismissive. As if he thought the janitorial staff should have put out traps for students like her. His attitude had always pissed her off, so she'd been the brash, pushy one—the one always in *his* face, refusing to let him forget that even though she was poor they'd once been friends.

"Torment is sort of subjective, don't you think?" she asked.

Brandon's eyebrows crept up under his bangs. The silent question was clear on his face.

She did another hand waggle. "Did he torment me, or did I torment him? It's a gray area."

"Oh, so it's like *that*."

"Like what?"

"Hey, I know high-school torture. There are no gray areas. High-school flirting on the other hand…there are about a thousand and one shades of sepia there."

Laney paused, wineglass halfway to her mouth. Brandon's breezy assessment had the effect of a freeze ray gun. After a moment's consideration, she tossed the last of her wine back in one gulp. It went down poorly, and she ended up damn near drowning in Malbec.

Brandon leaned forward to pat her on the back. "You okay?"

"Great," she choked, waving a hand in front of her face. "Peachy."

"Can I assume from your sudden inability to use your esophageal valve that you've never considered that possibility before?"

"No. I mean, yes. I'd never considered that. In high school, we hated each other. He treated me like I was trash, and I did everything I could to embarrass him."

Somehow, in her adolescent view of the world, there had been nothing but hatred and resentment there. But what if her assessment had been too simplistic? What if something else had been simmering beneath the surface of their antagonism and she'd just been too immature to notice it?

That certainly explained a lot. Particularly, her intense re-action to seeing him again after all this time.

She stared at her now-empty wineglass, suddenly wishing that she hadn't downed that last one so quickly, because she sure could use a bracing drink now.

"God, that sucks," she muttered aloud.

"Why?" Brandon asked, genuine and innocent confusion behind his curiosity. "Do you know how many people would kill for a chance at their high-school crush?"

"Right." She purposefully mimicked his pedantic tone. "And are you not considering one of the definitions of the word? They call it a crush because it's brutal and crippling. I don't think the fact that I was in denial is going to make it any less so."

"Good point."

She tipped her wineglass up, waiting patiently for the last drop of wine to shimmy into her mouth. "I think the best I can hope for here is a miracle." Maybe if Dalton realized how bad Gran's condition was, he'd back off. If Gran couldn't give him the info he needed, then surely the bargain would be off. Then he wouldn't give the money to the Woodland Theater, and she wouldn't have to feel as though she was bilking him. And as an added bonus, Dalton would be out of her life forever and she wouldn't have to see him again. Rather than try to explain all that to Brandon, she merely said, "Hopefully, this will all be over quickly. Then Dalton and I can both go on with our lives and no one need ever glance at the gray areas."

Brandon raised his glass in mock salute. "To ignoring the gray areas!"

Then he seemed to notice her glass was empty. He tipped his into hers, evening them out so she had enough for one more drink, which confirmed it. Best. Neighbor. Ever.

Matilda Fortino clearly was not having a good day. Dalton could see that from the expression on the receptionist's face the second he mentioned her name at the front desk.

The woman, whose name tag read Linda, just gave her head a sad little shake as she scrolled through the info on her computer screen. "And this is the first time you've visited Mrs. Fortino? Is that correct, Mr. Cain?"

"Yes, it is." Hoping Linda was just a naturally dour woman,

Dalton rolled forward onto the balls of his feet, eager to get on with the visit.

"I'll need to see your driver's license."

"I spoke with Laney Fortino just this morning. She said—"

"Oh, yes. You're cleared to visit. We scan everyone's license on their visit. It's for our records and allows us to print out our visitor passes."

He stifled his annoyance as he dug out his ID. He wasn't sure Cain Enterprises had security as good as the Restful Hills assisted-living facility.

While he waited for the receptionist to do her thing, he scanned the lobby. Restful Hills was a sprawling fenced-and-gated compound of buildings west of downtown, not far from the exclusive neighborhood where he'd grown up. The understated elegance of the lobby suggested a wealthy clientele with limitless resources—not exactly the kind of place he'd expected his parents' housekeeper to end up.

"Were you close to Mrs. Fortino?" Linda asked.

Dalton pulled his attention back to the receptionist and nodded. She seemed to be waiting for the computer to do something.

He frowned, questioning the woman's use of the past tense. "Were?"

The woman's smile took on a falsely bright glimmer as she ignored his question. "You haven't seen Mrs. Fortino recently, have you?"

"No."

Before he asked her anything else, a label printer churned out a visitor's pass, and Linda stood as she ripped it off.

"How bad is she?" he asked.

Instead of answering, Linda handed both the pass and his driver's license to him and gestured to the door behind her. "Mrs. Fortino is in room 327. According to the log, Ms. Fortino is with her now."

Okay, so the staff clearly couldn't talk about patients, and he hadn't really expected any indiscretion on Linda's part.

Still, he couldn't shake the feeling of unease. He was used to having all the information he needed at his fingertips, and it had been a long time since he'd walked into a meeting of any kind feeling completely unprepared.

He found the room easily enough. A middle-aged woman, either a doctor or an assistant, was leaving as he approached. She was dressed in scrubs and carried both a clipboard and a tablet.

The woman smiled and said softly, "You must be the visitor Laney is expecting. You can go on in." But then she placed a hand on his arm and added, "Mrs. Fortino doesn't always handle surprise well. You might want to take it easy this first time. You know, let Laney introduce you. That kind of thing."

He watched the woman retreat down the hall before entering through the still-open door. The apartment was small, no bigger than a standard business suite in a hotel. There was a kitchenette to the left of the door, an undersized refrigerator, microwave, dining table and sink. There was no cooktop or oven.

Straight ahead was a living area with a bathroom off to one side and a bedroom visible through an open doorway. Rather than the generic furniture of a hotel, the tiny apartment was decorated with a collection of older furniture—some antiques, some well-cared-for heirlooms. A crocheted throw had been draped over the back of the sofa.

Dalton realized with a jolt that he remembered it. He recognized it from one of the few times he'd visited the apartment over the carriage house where Mrs. Fortino had lived for so many years. Only then did he realize that this apartment must be only slightly smaller than that one had been. All of her furniture had fit into this tiny space, and it seemed only a little cramped.

In the center of the living area, facing a TV that was not on, sat one of the two dining-room chairs. Matilda Fortino sat in the chair, staring blankly at the TV. Laney sat on the arm of the sofa behind her, brushing out her grandmother's hair, which now fell past her waist.

When he entered, Laney glanced over her shoulder long enough to press the index finger of her free hand to her lips in a shushing gesture without ever slowing the rhythm of her brush strokes.

For several minutes, Laney brushed in silence. Then, speaking as softly as one would to an infant, she said, "I'm almost done with your hair, Mattie. Would you like me to braid it?"

"Is it Sunday?" Matilda asked.

He was used to hearing her talk in a brusque, no-nonsense tone. Even though he knew she wasn't wholly herself, it made him uncomfortable how uncertain she sounded.

"No," Laney murmured. "It's Saturday."

"You'll come back tomorrow, won't you, Elaine?"

"Of course."

Matilda twisted her hands. "Can we do it then?"

"We'll braid your hair whenever you want, honey."

Laney glanced back at him, smiling. It wasn't the mischievous grin he was used to seeing from her. It held none of that fire or spirit, but there was something sweet about it, something charming and nostalgic.

Laney set the brush aside and stroked her grandmother's hair several times with the palm of her hand. Then she gathered the hair and began to twist it into a knot. "You have a visitor today, if you'd like to see him."

"Is it one of my beaus?"

Dalton was so unused to hearing Mrs. Fortino like this. The woman he'd known had been strict and stern. There'd been nothing soft or girlish about her—nothing hesitant or uncertain.

"No. Just a friend." The knot began to take the shape of a bun. Laney plucked a hairpin from the table beside the sofa and secured the ends of the hair.

"Do I know him?"

"You knew him a long time ago. He's here now."

Matilda gave her hands another twist, then slowly turned to the door.

When she looked at him, Dalton had the feeling she'd known all along that he was there but had been slowly bracing herself for the encounter.

Confusion clouded her features—confusion and fear. Suddenly he understood. Despite the dreamy, girlish quality to her voice, some part of her knew she wasn't right. She knew she should know things she didn't. It wasn't strangers she dreaded; it was the not knowing.

She stood, her hands still knotting themselves in front of her. Laney got up as well, placing a steady hand on her grandmother's back.

"It's okay if you don't know him, Mattie. He was a boy the last time you saw him. This is Dalton. He's all grown up now."

"It's good to see you." He held out his hand and moved to step forward, but Laney gave her head a quick shake. Before he could stop the movement, Mrs. Fortino shrank back from him.

"No. I do know you." Revulsion crept into her voice, pushing aside all the girlishness. "I know those eyes. Those lies. You're a monster."

Five

Dalton had to brace himself against the hatred radiating from Mrs. Fortino's eyes.

"No, Gran, this isn't Hollister." Laney spoke quickly, grasping her grandmother by the arm. "This is his son, Dalton."

Mrs. Fortino swung her head around to look at Laney, the motion so fast, her hair tumbled out of its twist. "No, that Hollister is a devil. They all are. The Cains will destroy you." She grabbed Laney by the forearms and gave her a shake. "They'll destroy everything. He's a monster. You don't know what he's done. To his family. To his wife. He'll do it to you too. You should get out now. Just take the money and get out. Otherwise he'll destroy you."

Mrs. Fortino's hair was wild about her face as she shook Laney over and over. "He's a monster, and I can't just stand by and watch anymore."

Dalton's gut told him to propel himself across the room to protect Laney. But how was he supposed to protect her from her own grandmother? She was a woman in her eighties but still apparently strong.

"It's okay, Gran," Laney was saying over and over again. "It's okay. He's not going to hurt me. Hollister isn't here. You're okay."

Dalton looked around the room and found a call button on the wall. He slapped his hand on it, and a second later, it buzzed.

"Yes, Ms. Fortino?"

"We need help up here," he said.

"Right away, Mr. Cain."

"See?" Matilda demanded. "It is him. Even they know it. He can get to us anywhere. Is it safe? Have you hidden it? Like I asked you to? Did you hide it?"

"Please, Gran!" Laney's voice sounded desperate now. "Calm down! You have to calm down. Everything is okay."

Matilda stopped shaking Laney, but she tightened her hands on Laney's arms so that Laney cringed away, struggling to wrench herself free. "He will use you and destroy you, Vee. You need to get out while you can. Didn't you see what he did to Caroline and to Sharlene? He destroys them. You can't trust him."

"This isn't Hollister. This is Dalton. He's—"

"You think I don't know who he is." Matilda's gaze darted wildly around. "You think I'm crazy. Delusional. But I'm not! I know I'm not crazy!"

"Please, Gran, let go of me!"

As long as Matilda hadn't been hurting Laney, he'd been willing to wait for the staff to come in, but the second he saw real fear and pain flicker across Laney's face, he shot across the room and clamped his hands over Matilda's. She flinched away from him as if he'd hit her, releasing Laney as she dropped into a crouch, her arms sheltering her face.

An instant later, the door burst open and three orderlies rushed in. Laney, clearly shaken, started explaining what had happened.

"Sir," one of the orderlies said to him, "perhaps you should wait in the hall."

Laney was lowering herself to the edge of the sofa. One of the orderlies was tending Matilda; the other crouched down beside Laney. She met Dalton's gaze over the orderly's head and gave him a nod. Though clearly shaken, she was fine. And with the orderlies around, he felt confident Laney was safe and everything would be under control.

He left Matilda's apartment. After what he'd seen today, he could no longer think of her as Mrs. Fortino. That woman—with her strict rules and iron will—seemed gone forever. This other strangely vulnerable, borderline violent woman was someone else entirely.

For several minutes, Dalton just stood in the hall, staring at the door that had closed behind him. Then he pulled out his phone and checked his email. He called his assistant, even though it was Saturday. Thank goodness Sydney seemed to have no more of a life outside of work than he did. He would blame her recent breakup for her lack of social life, but she'd been just as focused on work before that. Just last week, he'd thought her total devotion to work completely natural. Now he wondered if perhaps he should feel guilty for bothering her on the weekend. She was young and beautiful and should be doing something fun on a Saturday. But he paid her very generously to be available around the clock. So he dictated a letter to her. Then he ended the call, and used his phone to catch up on all the sports news and was even scanning the entertainment headlines by the time the apartment door opened and Laney walked out. When she saw Dalton, she did a noticeable double take.

"You're still here."

He pushed up from the wall. "Yes."

She pressed her hand to her chest as if holding in her surprise. The strap of her purse was slung over her shoulder, and she clung to it like it was a lifeline. "I thought...or rather, I expected you to leave. I was going to call you later."

"Is she doing better?"

"Yes." Laney started walking down the hall, back toward the front office. He naturally fell into step beside her. "I know how surprising it is to see her like that. Sometimes she sees something that reminds her of the past or triggers a memory and she becomes agitated." They reached the hall that led to the main reception area and Laney paused. "The center has an on-site café. Do you want to get something? I could really use—"

"A stiff drink?"

"I was going to say a coffee." For the first time since leaving her grandmother's room, Laney smiled.

He felt the effect like a punch to the gut. It was the contrast, he decided: the cheerful smile against the high drama of dealing with Matilda. Anyone would feel knocked off balance.

But Laney seemed to tackle it all in stride—as if nothing about the experience with Matilda freaked her out.

He followed her down three more halls until they dead-ended in an elegant dining room. Small tables dotted the room, already set for the noon meal. Along the far wall, a coffee and tea station was set up. Laney dropped her purse on one of the tables and then walked to the coffee dispenser and poured herself a mug. At the far end of the room, a pair of double swing doors led to the kitchen. He could hear the kitchen staff starting the prep for lunch in the back. It was barely ten-thirty, but he suspected residents would start filtering down for lunch soon.

"The coffee is a little weak for my taste, but it's not bad."

"You drink a lot of it?"

"Enough."

"She's like that often?" He poured his own mug, waiting for her response.

"If you mean the total freak-out, that's pretty rare. Thank God, the staff knows how to handle it. I panicked the first time she did it."

"What usually sets her off?" Then he gestured to himself. "Besides demons from her past coming back to haunt her?"

Laney gave an exaggerated wince as she poured a healthy stream of sugar into her coffee. "Try not to take it personally."

"Hard not to."

"I'm sorry you had to see that."

"Don't feel like you have to apologize," he said. "It's like when parents on a plane feel bad because their baby is crying. It's not their fault. And it's not yours either. She's clearly very ill. And you had no way of knowing she'd react to me like that."

She shook her head as she plucked a napkin from the dispenser and carefully wrapped it around her cup, then stirred the mixture with a tiny straw. Maybe it was the way she kept her head ducked or maybe it was her complete and total focus on such a simple task, but there was guilt in her posture.

"I guess." Then she tossed the straw into the nearby trash can and straightened her shoulders before pulling out a chair from one of the nearby tables. "No. I did know. Not that she'd totally freak out, but I knew she wasn't having a good day."

He had a lot of questions about Matilda's health, but he didn't want Laney to mistake his concern for rubbernecking. So he sipped his coffee, waiting for her to fill in the gaps for him if she wanted to talk.

Apparently she did, because she went to sit at the table where she set her purse down, cradling her mug in her hands. Once he sat down opposite her, she started talking.

"Some days, she's fine. Almost like her old self. Marching around that tiny apartment and complaining that I don't visit often enough or about the inferior job the staff does cleaning. On the really bad days, she doesn't even know I'm there."

"And on days like this?" he prodded.

"Days like today, she seems to drift in and out of the past." Laney seemed unable to meet his gaze. Instead she toyed with the edge of the napkin she'd wrapped around her coffee cup. "She rambles a lot and sometimes she doesn't make any sense.

Other times she seems not to know me at all. She gets upset if I call her Gran, because she doesn't even remember having a granddaughter. Or she'll call me Elaine, like she did just now."

"I thought Elaine was your given name."

"Well, sure, but no one's ever called me that. Elaine was her sister. They had a falling out when they were young and didn't speak for years. And then Elaine died young. In her twenties, I think." Laney took another sip but then set her cup down with resolve, as if she'd decided she'd had enough of feeling sorry for herself. "I should have known better than to have you come out today. Days like today, she's more fragile."

And yet, in that moment, it was Laney herself who seemed fragile. Laney, who had always been such a fireball of defiance. Laney, who had never backed down from a fight in her life. Laney seemed as emotionally frail as a butterfly, delicate and ephemeral. He'd read once that if you touched a butterfly's wings, it would never again be able to fly.

Maybe that was why he didn't reach for Laney, then, even though he desperately wanted to pull her into his arms. Even though he wanted to comfort her almost as much as he wanted to kiss her.

So he didn't comfort her and he didn't press her for more information, even though his mind raced with questions about Matilda's breakdown. Why had she called Laney "Vee"? Did Laney know anything about the money Matilda mentioned? Or was the entire rant just the raving of a tortured mind? They were questions he didn't ask. Laney had been visibly shaken by the experience. He wouldn't make it worse just to satisfy his curiosity.

Instead, he said, "Nonsense. You couldn't have known how she would react."

Laney cut her eyes to him, her expression annoyed. "I'll feel bad about it if I want to. And for the record, I feel bad for putting her through that, not for inconveniencing you. But—" she seemed to force herself to meet his gaze "—I knew you wouldn't get the information you needed. Not today. The truth is, I wanted to make this hard on you. I was hoping you'd give up once you saw how bad off she is."

"I see." He eyed her for a few moments in silence.

Funny, the game playing didn't surprise him as much as her honesty did. Everyone he knew had ulterior motives, but almost no one owned up to them. The vulnerability in her honesty nearly made him ache. The urge to protect Laney surprised him. He wasn't used to letting anything or anyone get in the way of his goals. What was it about Laney that made him act in ways so completely against his nature?

Suddenly, he felt like an ass for not being completely honest himself. "Well, if we're being honest, I was never really sure she could help."

Laney gave a tiny flinch of surprise. A frown settled on her face as she cocked her head, studying him. "If you didn't think she could help, then why go to all this trouble? Why bother?"

Laney bristled as she asked the question, suddenly more cat than butterfly. But of course, she was neither. Laney was all woman. She was smart and perceptive and there was no point playing games. Eventually, she'd see right through whatever excuses he offered up.

"Once I found out she was sick, I honestly didn't expect to find out anything," he admitted.

"Then why come out today?"

He leaned back in his chair and studied Laney, taking in her wary expression. For too long, she'd looked at him like this, her large amber eyes filled with distrust and suspicion. As if he was her enemy instead of her friend. But in the back of his mind was the image of Laney as she'd once been: his friend. In the brief time she'd been back in his life, he'd caught mere glimpses of that other Laney, the one he remembered from their teenage years. The one filled with warmth and affection. The one who smiled easily and who laughed with abandon.

He wanted to see more of that Laney. He wanted her back in his life. Who was he kidding? He just wanted her. He had for years. And if the spark of awareness in her eyes was any indication, she wanted him too, even if she wasn't ready to let herself admit it yet.

Yes, with everything else going on in his life, the timing wasn't good, but he wasn't going to let that get in his way. Even though he'd never approved of his father's business tactics, he and his father did have one thing in common. When they wanted something, they got it.

Laney may not know it yet, but she was his.

He smiled slowly as he said, "Because I wanted to see you again."

Laney didn't think of herself as a naturally nervous person, but there was something about the look Dalton gave her that made her skin tingle and her nerves all but jump. The smile he gave her was heated and predatory. Dark and dangerous. It made something inside her leap in alarm.

She'd heard about snakes that hypnotize their prey with the intensity of their gaze. That's how she felt. Pinned to the spot, unable to move, hypnotized by the sensual promise in Dalton's eyes.

Part of her knew she should be relieved. His words—not to mention his blatant perusal—implied he was more interested in her body than in Gran's possible felonious behavior or her own amateur attempts at distraction. She should be mopping her brow with relief. Instead, her pulse quickened and she could barely pull enough air into her lungs to keep up.

This must be what a fluffy little lemur felt like moments before the python slithered off the branch above it and swallowed it whole. Dalton had that kind of power—the ability to devour her completely, body and soul. And she wasn't sure she had the strength to resist. She did, however, have more sense than a fluffy lemur. She wasn't just going to sit and let herself be hypnotized when she could scurry to safety.

Unable to contain her nerves, she jumped up. "You know what? I think we should go." Her words poured out in a rush. "We're done here, right? So we should go."

A slow, predatory smile spread across his face. Who knew snakes could smile?

She edged back an inch. "What?"

"I make you nervous, don't I?"

"No." She let out a *phft* of denial. "Of course not." 'Cause lemurs always looked so relaxed. "I just need to go. I mean, I have things to do today."

He stood, then pushed in his chair. "Of course you do." He carried his coffee mug and hers over to the busing station and then nodded toward the cafeteria. "I'm sure you're very busy."

"I am!" she protested. "My theater group meets every Saturday at two. And that's—" she glanced at her watch...three hours away "—well, I have to go home and shower first. I need to make lunch. I have a lot to do between now and then."

How bad would it look if she bolted for the door? Would it be any worse than standing here babbling like an idiot? It was hard to imagine it would.

She turned and started walking toward the lobby, even though she knew he wouldn't let her retreat so easily.

"I do make you nervous—"

"No! You don't."

"Then why would you be running away?"

Ah, crap. Why had Dalton been blessed with good looks and brains?

"I'm not running. I'm just busy," she quipped as she entered the lobby, trying to steer Dalton away from Linda's desk.

"Then let me drive you home."

"No, of course not," she hissed, automatically stepping closer to him so she could whisper, "Don't be ridiculous." To Linda she said, "I'll see you tomorrow."

"I heard your grandmother had a tough time of it today," Linda said with a sympathetic head tilt. Of course, strictly speaking, the staff wasn't allowed to talk about the patients, but three orderlies rushing down the hall to sedate someone was hard not to notice. "I'm sorry."

Linda's gaze bumped back and forth between Laney and Dalton.

Dalton noticed too, and Laney saw the instant he decided to use Linda to get his way. "You're still upset," Dalton said to Laney, his tone solicitous.

Laney jerked her gaze to him, glaring daggers.

"About your grandmother." He reached over and took her arm in his, raising it up to show Linda. "Look at her, she's still shaking."

To Laney's surprise, he was right. A visible tremor went through her hand. She hadn't even noticed. But of course it wasn't what had happened with her grandmother that had her shaking. It was their conversation afterward that had affected her.

"I should drive you," he said.

"I'm fine." She whipped her hand away. "I certainly don't need you to drive me."

Dalton ignored her and spoke to Linda. "She won't listen to me. Maybe you can talk her into accepting a ride. Besides, I don't think she should be alone right now."

Before Laney could protest, Linda had rounded the counter and pulled Laney into a hug. "You poor thing. The day you've had. And you still have your Saturday class." Linda clucked her disapproval.

"Yes," Laney said stiffly, again glaring daggers at Dalton over Linda's shoulder. "And I'm already late."

"Laney, dear—" Linda gave Laney's back several reassuring pats "—you do too much. Believe me, I know. I'm the same way. But sometimes you've just got to let other people help you."

Laney was furious with Dalton. The bastard had engineered this situation masterfully. He'd backed her into a corner, and now she had to accept the ride from him. Damn it!

Three days ago, she'd barely remembered that Dalton Cain even existed. Now he'd washed into her life like a tidal wave, and she could hardly see over the crest of the water.

She forced her lips into a smile. "Well, when you put it that way, I don't suppose I have any choice." She glanced at Dalton. "Do I?"

"No, you don't." His own smile looked much more natural—if the lion looking at the mouse under his paw could smile, that is.

"What am I supposed to do about my car?" she asked pointedly, making one last grasp for the life preserver floating back out to sea.

"I'll send a driver to pick it up and bring it by your place. You leave your keys here with Linda, and you'll have your car back within the hour."

Linda clapped her hands together. "See? Perfect solution! And this way you won't have to drive while you're upset."

Dalton gave Laney's arm a squeeze and then headed out the door. "Wait here while I pull around the car."

When Dalton disappeared from view, Laney turned around to find Linda watching her.

"What a nice young man." Linda practically beamed.

Laney held back a derisive snort but just barely. Dalton was about as nice as a tornado. He had the power to transport her to another world or to crush her mercilessly. She wasn't sure if he cared one way or the other.

"He certainly seems fond of you," Linda added, with a broad grin and waggling eyebrows.

"Yes, he does, doesn't he," Laney murmured with a tight smile.

That was the key point, wasn't it? He *seemed* fond of her. But she knew better than to be fooled by that. When she was thirteen, Dalton had seemed like her best friend, until, oops, he wasn't anymore. She wasn't going to make that mistake again.

"If you don't mind my saying, dear, I think you could use the diversion that a man like him could provide."

Laney bit her tongue to hold back her response. She so

didn't need anything Dalton could provide. Unless it was a Get Out of Jail Free card.

Thank God, at that moment Laney saw Dalton's cream Lexus pull around under the front portico. She bolted for the door, desperate to escape from Linda's advice.

She clambered into the passenger seat of Dalton's car and slammed the door behind her. But of course, it was a case of out of the frying pan and into the fire if there ever was one. She was no longer at the mercy of Linda's matchmaking attempts—or whatever that could be called. But now she was trapped in the car for thirty minutes with Dalton.

Inside, the sedan epitomized understated luxury, all smooth leather and sleek chrome. The interior was so pristine that she might have thought he'd driven it off the lot that very morning, except it didn't have the new-car smell. Instead it smelled like Dalton: woodsy and masculine. And though the smell itself wasn't overpowering, the effect was. It was like being trapped inside his shirt pocket.

It wasn't so much into the fire as into the nuclear reactor.

Dalton shot her a look. "You okay?"

Laney's eyebrows shot up in disbelief. "Seriously?"

"What?" He'd returned his gaze to the road as he pulled out into the Houston traffic, which was always a mess, even on a Saturday morning.

"Don't pretend to be concerned about me."

"Why wouldn't I be?"

"Dalton, the only thing you're concerned about is getting what you want. You manipulated poor Linda." Poor Linda. Jeez. The woman had practically thrown her into his arms. The phrase *poor Linda* was an outright lie. And all Laney needed was to be struck by lightning while in the nuclear reactor. "The point is, you'll say or do anything to get what you want and—"

"Yes."

She broke off and stared at him. "What?"

"Yes, I will." He glanced at her for only a second before

returning his attention to the road. He maneuvered the car through traffic and onto the ramp of Highway 10. His Lexus hummed powerfully as it zipped through traffic. "Surely that doesn't shock you."

"I—" She glanced down to see her hand knitted around the strap of her purse. "No. It doesn't."

"Good."

His tone was thick with some emotion she couldn't name—something she couldn't identify that made her deeply uncomfortable.

"I—" she started again, but again she broke off. She didn't know what to say to him—didn't know how to feel—didn't know how to process this sudden new vulnerability.

Finally, she twisted to face him, bringing her leg up onto the seat beside her. "I can't let you bully me, Dalton Cain."

He frowned. "I have enough people in my life who let me bully them. I have employees who jump every time I so much as twitch. But I know you won't let me bully you. I never expected you to."

His voice was softer now—more intimate. And she knew instantly that he was telling the truth…that he didn't plan to bully her. That he never expected to get away with it—not with her.

Why did that disconcert her more than anything else?

Maybe because it told her something about how he saw her, not as one of his subjects but as an equal.

She shifted in her seat again—this time to stare out the window. The Houston cityscape passed by unnoticed.

They didn't talk for the remainder of the drive. She didn't pay attention to his driving but instead focused on sorting through her thoughts.

Too many things had happened in the past few hours for her to be able to easily process any of it. This morning, her plan had seemed so simple. Let him get a glimpse of Gran at her worst, he'd understand that Gran couldn't help him, then he'd back off, leaving them alone without ever having discov-

ered Gran's perfidy. Easy peasy. He should have left as soon
as Gran freaked out.

Instead, he'd hung around. He'd been all nice. He'd tried to
comfort her, the bastard. And then she'd spilled her guts, idiot
that she was. And now, here they were. His intentions were
obviously lascivious, which was just intolerable.

There was absolutely no way she was getting involved with
him—not when she so desperately needed to get him out of
her life.

And then she remembered she still had to tell him that
she couldn't accept the donation to Woodland Theater. Sure,
she'd never really had any intention of keeping it. The money
had only ever been an attempt to distract him. One that had
failed anyway.

Of course, she still couldn't tell him the real reason she
hadn't wanted him to talk to Gran. And now he would assume
she was putting him off to avoid dealing with the chemistry
between them.

The really bad thing was, she wasn't sure he'd be wrong.

Six

Sitting beside him in the car, Laney was unnaturally still and quiet. He could almost see the storm cloud brewing over her head. Then, she abruptly muttered a colorful curse.

"Excuse me?" he said, surprised but somehow pleased as well. The Laney he'd once known—that eleven-year-old tomboy who had climbed up the outside of the house to sneak into his bedroom window so he could teach her chess late at night—had cussed like a Russian mobster. He liked being reminded that that girl still existed.

"I was just thinking about the money."

"Thinking about money makes you curse?"

"Not money. *The* money," she explained, like that was supposed to clarify things. "The money you donated to the Woodland Theater."

"And that upsets you because…?"

"Isn't it obvious? Gran can't help you find the heiress. I never should have accepted the money knowing—"

"You didn't *accept* the money," he pointed out, smiling. "You *demanded* it."

Clearly not amused, she grumbled, "Fine. I never should have *demanded* the money, since you clearly didn't know how bad Gran was doing and I did." She crossed her arms over her chest and fumed. "It's your fault, really. You're so pushy."

She looked petulant, disgruntled and so damned cute it was all he could do not to chuckle. "Fine. I accept full blame."

"That doesn't change anything. Because Gran still can't help you, so I still have to return the money." She sighed, sounding dejected. "It was nice, pretending for a few days that I didn't have to worry about money."

"So keep the money."

"Yeah. Right."

"Why not?" he asked.

The look she sent him seemed to question his sanity or his intelligence—or both. Probably both.

"I can't keep the money. Not if Gran can't help you."

"So, we'll try again in a few days. Sometime when she's doing better."

"There are no guarantees that she'll have a good day," Laney pointed out. "You saw the way she reacted to you. I can't risk putting her through that again."

"I wouldn't ask you to." Yes, he needed to find out anything she might know, but not at that cost. He'd seen the defeated exhaustion on Laney's face when she'd walked out of her grandmother's room. He wouldn't put either of them through that again.

"Why not keep the money? You asked for it knowing Matilda probably couldn't help. I gave it to you knowing she might not be able to. Yes, I need to find the heiress, but if you can't help me find her, I still want to see you."

She stared at him blankly for a moment and then held up her palms as if warding off a leper. "Are you saying you're paying me to spend time with you? Because, eww. That so does not make it better."

"You know that's not what I meant."

"It better not be."

"Tell me something. Why do you care so much about this Woodland Theater group of yours? You give up evenings and weekends for this. From what I've seen, you work your butt off. Why bother?"

"Why bother?" she repeated, twisting in her seat to look at him. Passion and enthusiasm lit her normally wary eyes. "The kids who are in class, they all need this. Sure, there are other afterschool programs, but not like this one. I sell the program to their parents by telling them that acting increases confidence and helps with public speaking. But that's not why these kids need it. They need the chance to escape their lives for a while. To be someone else. Kids—particularly these private-school kids from Tisdale—they never really have a chance to just be kids. They're pressured to succeed from the cradle."

He felt Laney's attention on him. "Yeah. I know something about that."

She shifted in her seat so that she was looking out the front window. "Yeah. I suspect you do."

"But you work hard for the Woodland Theater, right? To make sure these kids have a chance to really be kids?"

"Of course." She sounded insulted that he might think otherwise.

"And the kids get a lot out of it?"

"They do," she admitted, her pride obvious.

"Then accept the money." She looked like she wanted to protest, but he didn't give her a chance. "As you pointed out, I'll hardly miss it."

Traffic on the highway had slowed to a crawl, as it did so often in Houston, and he took the opportunity to study her again. She was frowning, like he hadn't really convinced her. He wasn't entirely sure why it was suddenly so important to him that she keep the money. After all, the Cains weren't known for their generosity. The Cains donated to charitable organizations for tax purposes and at the suggestion of their

CPAs. They picked organizations that would sculpt the company's public profile. They did not impulsively donate a hundred grand to children's theater groups. So what exactly was he doing here?

"You should take the money," he repeated. "You'll earn it."

But he wondered suddenly if he was trying to convince her or himself.

Then Laney gave a jerk of excitement, as though someone had plugged her finger in a socket. "Or I *could* earn it!"

"Isn't that what I said?"

She shifted, pulling her knee up on the seat and turning to face him. "No, I mean, I could help you find the heiress."

"Laney—"

"No, I'm serious! It'll be a finder's fee or something. If I help you find the missing heiress, then I won't feel weird about you donating the money. You'll have absolutely no reason to talk to Gran again. And once this is over, we'll never have to see each other again. Everything will be perfect."

He saw the exit for her neighborhood and darted through traffic to make it, using the snarl on the highway as an excuse not to respond right away as he considered her offer. Was he really ready to have her help him search for the missing heiress? If not, then what exactly was he doing here?

Seeing her again, wanting to spend time with her, was one thing. Having her dig around in the darkest and dirtiest of the Cain closets was something else entirely. Suddenly, he didn't want her marred by the nastiness of whatever skeletons this search was going to bring up.

And he didn't even want to think about that land mine she'd dropped at the end of her perfect plan—the part about not ever seeing him again.

"Is it really so awful?" he asked before he could think better of it. "Having to deal with me again?"

Her gaze jerked to his in surprise, then she let out a bark of laughter. "Oh, poor baby," she teased, bumping her elbow against his playfully. "Did I hurt your feelings?"

"I'm serious." It surprised him that he meant it. Why was he serious? Why did it matter to him what she thought?

She gave another chuckle, shaking her head in exasperation. "It can't shock you that I don't exactly want to start a book club with you or become golf buddies or—"

"No offense to your taste in books or your golfing skills, but neither of those things are exactly what I had in mind."

"Yeah, well, I was speaking euphemistically. But I don't want to do any of the noneuphemistic things either."

But he could tell by the way her gaze darted away from his that she wasn't exactly telling the truth. So he backed up and approached from another angle. "Come on, Laney. We were friends once."

"And then we weren't," she said sharply. "And we've been not friends a lot longer than we were friends. I guess I'm too used to the status quo."

Yeah. That whole not-friends thing had tripped him up too. The friends part was the easy thing. He'd been thirteen the summer she came to live with Matilda. To be honest, he'd been a brat—already convinced of his own importance. Why wouldn't he be when he'd had Hollister already molding him into the next leader of Cain Enterprises?

But Laney hadn't taken any of his crap, not even back then. She'd been this awkward, scrawny tomboy with haunted eyes, a propensity for getting in trouble and more guts than all the rest of them combined. He never intended to befriend her, but he hadn't seemed to have much of a choice. As long as they'd been just friends, everything was fine.

But then she hit puberty, just before starting high school, and suddenly everything had changed. He'd wanted her. He'd wanted her with the crazy, pent-up lust of a teenage boy. He'd wanted her because she drove him crazy because she was constantly underfoot, inescapably nearby yet forever out of reach.

At the time, he'd known with absolute certainty that he couldn't have her. He couldn't so much as touch her. If he slept with her and his mother found out, Laney and her grandmother both would have been kicked to the curb. Any sort of emotional entanglement would have been even worse. If his father had thought he was in love with her, Hollister wouldn't have been content to fire Matilda and kick them both out. Hollister would have crushed them—destroyed them completely.

When they were young, pursuing her hadn't been an option. He'd stayed away to protect her. But he'd been a teenager and hadn't had the emotional maturity to *just* stay away. He'd never been able to *just* ignore her. He'd had to work at it—to push her away.

She wasn't the type to take that, though. She'd pushed back. She'd poked and prodded and teased him. She'd done everything she could to work her way under his skin. And the harder she'd worked to irritate him, the harder it had become to freeze her out.

But he'd managed it because it had been the only way to protect her.

It occurred to him now, sitting here, alone with her, that she no longer needed his protection—not from his family at least. His parents could do nothing to hurt her.

There was nothing to keep him from pursuing Laney Fortino.

Dalton was strangely quiet as he followed her directions through her neighborhood to drop her off. She hoped rather than believed that she'd stumped him and that this was his way of backing off. It wasn't until he'd walked her up her front steps that he asked, "So when am I going to see you again?"

"Well, I'm free tomorrow afternoon. Where should we start? Does your father have any personal records? Maybe a journal?"

"No, that's not what I meant. I meant, when can I see you again?"

The sensual promise in his words skittered over her nerves like a physical caress. It scared the hell out of her, even as it turned her on. "Dalton…"

But he reached for her, refusing to let her retreat too far, and before she knew it, her back was pressed against her door and his fingers were inching up her arm. "Come on, Laney, you can't tell me you're immune to this. You can't pretend there's nothing between us."

"Don't." She held up a hand, warding him off before he could step any closer. "I'm not going to play these games just to stroke your ego."

"Maybe it's not my ego I'm worried about."

The very tone of his voice, pitched low and intimate, sent heat spiraling through her body, and she stepped forward slightly. She looked at the spot on her arm where his hand rested and then forced her gaze back up to his face.

She actually felt her heart skip a beat. God, he was so handsome—heartbreakingly, epically handsome. It killed her sometimes that a man who looked so hot could be so cold inside. It was one of those great cosmic jokes—like the way the sun could shine bright on bitterly cold days and the way lightning storms could be both beautiful and deadly.

No man should be so sexy and so heartless at the same time. And she should not have to work this hard to remind herself that he was the very last thing she wanted.

She pointedly looked him up and down and then shook his hand off her arm. "I'm not worried about any of your body parts."

His lips twitched like he was trying to suppress a smile. "Not even my heart?"

She glanced back up at his face, prepared to make a joke, maybe to rap on his chest and listen for the hollow sound, but his expression stopped her. He wasn't smiling anymore. He wasn't laughing—and he didn't appear to be teasing.

He was just watching her. His expression was intense and hot as though he wanted nothing more than to devour her whole.

Her breath caught in her chest, like a little bubble of hope. She swallowed it back. She couldn't let herself feel anything when it came to Dalton, especially not hope. Hope was a gateway drug. It led to other, far more dangerous emotions, like love. And then anguish.

She'd rather cut herself off now. She'd already been through the Dalton Cain recovery program. She couldn't afford to do it a second time.

"No. Especially not your heart. I'm pretty sure that particular organ shriveled up and died sometime during my freshman year."

"Is that what you really believe?"

She blew out a frustrated breath. "What do you want me to say? You can't really expect me to pretend that you didn't treat me like dirt that year." He started to say something, but she held up a hand, cutting him off. "Look, I get it. Teenagers are selfish and cruel. They value the opinions of their peers, and they make rash decisions. So you were okay being my best friend in private but not at school. You were okay having the little poor girl be your friend at home, as long as none of your friends knew about it. But as soon as I started going to the same high school as you that was over. We were done. I get it. I'm even over it. I forgive you or whatever you need to hear. But I'm not going to pretend it didn't happen. I'm not going to just let you back into my life like you never betrayed me."

"Is that really what you thought?"

She wanted to flee into the house, to slam the door on him and never see him again. Ninety-nine percent of her knew that was the only right thing to do. But there was still that one percent of her—that fourteen-year-old girl who started high school expecting her friend to be there with her. That fourteen-year-old girl had been scared as hell on their first day of school, knowing she was poorer than almost everyone else there. Knowing she was outclassed and undereducated. Knowing she couldn't have even gotten into the exclusive private school if not for the Cains' munificence. The one thing she'd clung to was knowing her best friend would be there too. Then that same guy had turned his back on her and ignored her.

That fourteen-year-old girl wanted answers.

No, not answers. She knew the answers. She wanted retribution.

"What was I supposed to think, Dalton?" She propped her hands on her hips. "For two years, you and I were friends. We hung out after school and over the summers. But the second I started high school that ended. You shut me out."

"You think I stopped hanging out with you because you were too young?"

"I don't think it had anything to do with my age. You stopped being my friend because I was poor. I was just white trash who wasn't good enough to be your friend."

"That's where you're wrong. You and I could never have been friends in high school."

"Right. Because I wasn't good enough."

"No. We weren't friends because I was never going to be happy being *just* your friend."

His words surprised her so much she rocked back a step. "What?"

He followed her, closing the distance between them until she was backed against her door again with every line of trim biting into her skin.

"The only reason we were friends for the first couple of years you lived with your grandmother is because I was too young to understand what I really felt for you."

At his words, her lungs stopped working. Literally, she couldn't pull air into her body. So it was amazing that she had enough breath to ask, "What was it you felt?"

"Come on. You're going to make me spell it out?"

All she could muster was a nod.

"Two teenagers living so close together? It's amazing nothing did happen between us. I was sixteen and you were—" He broke off, seeming to struggle for words. Then he reached up to tuck a strand of hair behind her ear. He drew his knuckle across her cheek. "And you were so damn beautiful. For three years, I went to sleep every night knowing you were five-hundred feet away. It damn near killed me being that close to you and not having you."

Finally her lungs started working again. It was either that or pass out entirely. But by the time she started breathing again, he'd chucked her on the chin and turned to walk back to the car.

Laney stared at him for a minute, dumbfounded. Then she chased after him.

Laney came after him, her jaw set in a stubborn angle that declared she was on the offensive. He knew the expression well from her teenage years. Any sane man would tremble in his boots at her expression, but instead, Dalton's body leaped in response.

He didn't want Laney cowering away from him. He wanted her sass. He wanted her refusing to back down. That was the Laney he remembered.

He smiled when she stopped in front of him, hands propped on her hips.

"So what exactly did you think was going to happen here?"

"I don't know what you're talking about," he said, feigning innocence.

"I'm talking about that big revelation of yours. What did you hope to gain by telling me how you felt in high school? What exactly were you trying to accomplish?"

"Because naturally, you assume I have an ulterior motive."

"Exactly. You don't reveal any kind of vulnerability unless you think you can get something in return. So what did you think was going to happen? Did you think you'd spill your guts, tell me this big dark secret, and then…what? Did you think I'd fall into your arms and we'd have crazy, passionate sex?"

Her words wound through his brain, lighting his nerve endings on fire. He had to push his answer out past a lump in his throat. "No."

Before he could offer her any more of an explanation, she

launched herself into his arms. He staggered back, automatically wrapping his arms around her.

She looked up at him, her hands twining through his hair. "Because, actually, I think that would be a great idea."

Then she gave his head a tug and pulled his lips toward hers.

He resisted for only a fraction of a second—and then only because it seemed wrong, somehow, to be kissing her now so soon after getting her back in his life.

After waiting so many years, kissing Laney should be…an event. He didn't want this to be some quick, mindless peck. He wanted to sear it into his memory. Into hers.

He'd only ever kiss her for the first time once. And…

Ah, hell. Screw it.

Her body was pressed to his. Her lips were mere millimeters away. He couldn't wait anymore.

His mouth found hers. Her lips felt as though they'd been made for him to kiss—a divine combination of silky soft skin, sun-kissed warmth and Laney.

Just Laney.

She was warm and tasted sweet. And the moment her mouth opened to his, the instant her tongue stroked hungrily against his, it was like fireworks going off in his head.

His hands found the tantalizing flesh of her buttocks, and he pulled her even tighter against him. She came to him eagerly, one leg hitching up the outside of his hip.

He spun her around and backed her up. One step. Then another and another until he felt her legs bump against the hood of his car. From there, there was nowhere to go but down.

Everything about her was intoxicating: the taste of her skin on his lips, the scent of her, the twitchy way she bumped against him. It was as if she couldn't get enough of the feel of his body against hers—as if she was ready to take him right here—in front of her house, in broad daylight. It was as if she couldn't wait another minute.

Her fingers had abandoned his hair and moved down to

tug at the buttons of his shirt. Her hands were hot and eager against his skin, but every touch of her fingers ratcheted up his blood pressure. The pounding in his brain seemed to grow louder and louder, and it demanded that he speed this up. That he take her now—fast and hard.

But he didn't want fast and hard. He wanted slow and hot. He wanted mind-blowing. And if she kept touching him, it wasn't his mind that was going to blow.

He grabbed her hands and dragged them off his chest. He pinned them on either side of her shoulders as he trailed kisses across her jawbone to her neck. She groaned, bucking against him in a way that drove him mad.

Kissing her, feeling her against him, tasting her skin, was everything he'd ever dreamed of.

Just seeing her like this, splayed out across the hood of his car, was an adolescent wet dream come true.

She was going to drive him mad.

And she was going to be pissed as hell.

He released her hands and used his own to lever himself up off the car. He brought her with him, holding her body hard against his as he stood, then slowly lowering her to her feet. Only then did he lift his head.

He met her gaze without quite releasing her. Her eyes were wide, her expression stunned.

It took him a few ragged breaths before he had enough air to speak. That was okay. It took him almost that long before he knew what to say—and twice that long to overcome his own body's protests.

"Nice try, Laney," he finally said.

She blinked. "Huh?"

He gave her delectable ass one last squeeze, then set her away from him. "I'm guessing you figured we could just dive right in. Cut through the sexual tension and get it all over with."

Her shirt had ridden up, exposing a tempting swath of tummy. She tugged self-consciously at it. "I… Yeah. Isn't that what I...?" But by then, she must have seen the keys he was fishing out of his pocket, because her voice rose sharply as she asked, "You're leaving?"

He nodded, rounding to the driver's side of the car before he could talk himself out of it. "As tempting as this is—" and, boy, she had no idea how tempting it was "—you're going to have to work a little harder than this."

She followed him around the car and stood on the other side of the door as he swung it open. "You're leaving?" she demanded a second time. "I just threw myself at you, and you're walking away?"

"Not walking away. Biding my time."

Somehow, everything had changed in the past seventy-two hours. Because that's what Laney did to him. She turned his life upside down. She'd done it when she was eleven. He should have known she'd do it as an adult.

He hadn't lied when he'd told her he didn't expect them to have sex. He may have wanted all of those things, but he owed her more than that. Yes, he was coming after her, but he wasn't going to do it now. Because she deserved more than a half-assed pursuit while he was distracted by this nonsense with the Cain heiress. Laney deserved to be the focus of his attention. She deserved to be the center of his universe.

He nearly laughed at the expression of exasperation on her face. "I've been waiting sixteen years for this," he told her. "I can wait a few more days."

Seven

Laney watched, dumbfounded, as Dalton climbed into his car and drove away. After all his big talk, she'd expected him to try to press his advantage. She'd expected him to make a move.

Surely she wasn't disappointed that he hadn't?

How crazy would that be?

Okay, so he'd dropped this big bomb about how he'd felt in high school only to…no, *felt* wasn't the right word. *Felt* implied emotions. He hadn't said a word about feelings. He'd spoken of desire…of purely physical sensation—of lust.

Except this was Dalton. *Dalton.*

He'd been her friend and her nemesis. She'd adored him, been crushed by him, pined for him, hated him.

Was something as simple as lust possible, or would the complicated jumble of emotion she'd felt in the past bleed into the present?

Lust she could handle. Anything more complicated than that felt like quicksand. Oh, sure, on the surface love looked solid and stable—like the kind of beautiful sandy beach where you'd want to spread out your beach towel and just spend the rest of your life. But in her experience, all that gorgeous sand was just a thin layer over a sinkhole that would swallow you whole.

She'd spent her entire life avoiding that trap.

If this was any other time in her life, if Dalton was any other man, this would be her cue to pack up her bags and move. But that wasn't possible now. She had a job she loved, kids who depended on her, and Gran. No way was she leaving Gran alone.

And this was Dalton. Booting him out of her life wasn't an option. She knew the kind of man he was, both in his personal life and his professional life. When he wanted something, he went after it. He didn't give up until he had what he wanted. And unless she was mistaken, he wanted her.

And to make matters even more complicated, she'd just demanded that he let her spend more time with him. What was wrong with her? Was she insane?

If he was coming after her, how long would she have the strength to deny him?

This was about sex, pure and simple.

The way she saw it she had two options. The first was to try to hold her ground. She could throw up as many defenses against him as she could and pray like hell that she could weather the storm. Or she could go on the offensive—go after him as hard and as fast as he'd come at her and hope that they both got this out of their systems before he found out about the money Gran had stolen and before her emotions got too muddled.

Laney spent her entire Sunday brooding about Dalton. Yes...brooding. She was woman enough to admit that.

She woke early, even though it was normally the one morning a week she could sleep in. Little things like sleep were easier to do when you weren't haunted by the ghosts of boyfriends past. Instead, she caught up on her laundry and then finished her grading. She then even had time to tidy up the living room and vacuum, tasks that normally only got done during school holidays.

And it was still before nine when she climbed into her car to drive to Restful Hills. A driver had dropped it off and brought her the keys the previous evening. Now, she got into the car and sniffed suspiciously. Then she ran her finger across the dash. It came away clean. She poked at the tote bag of school junk she usually carted around with her. Yes, all the detritus of her life was where she normally kept it—the tote bag, the phone charger, her sunglasses, were all where they were supposed to be. Her iPod was still queued up to the classic jazz she loved best. But the floorboard was mysteriously clean of Jack in the Box bags and the dash was dust free. Someone had detailed her car.

She started it up and watched as the needle on the gas gauge crept over to full. And gassed it.

Maybe this was just standard operating procedure when you had a driver. Hell, she didn't know because she was just a normal middle-class person. Okay, low to middle. Whatever.

Maybe the white-glove treatment shouldn't have annoyed her, but it kind of did. Not because she didn't like it—hell, she could get used to never having to gas up her car—but because she knew there were some mighty long strings attached to those white gloves.

And she was used to being one-hundred percent string free.

She was used to taking care of herself not because she liked it that way but because that's how it had to be. Her father had died when she was eleven. And her wild-child mother had been out of the picture long before that. She'd been on her own. Yeah, sure, she'd had Gran, but Gran had never been the warm, fuzzy sort. So even though she'd had all her physical needs met, emotionally speaking, she'd been on her own. She was used to her independence. She couldn't afford to get used to having someone take care of her, because she knew it wouldn't last for long.

Determined not to let a full gas tank ruin her day, Laney stopped by her favorite bagel spot on the way to visit Matilda. She even defiantly threw the wrapper on the floorboard as she popped the last bite in her mouth.

Laney signed in at the front desk and rushed for the elevator before Linda could strike up a conversation. She wasn't sure she could take another one of her Dalton's-so-dreamy speeches.

Which meant she didn't know what mood to expect when she knocked on Gran's door. Sometimes, after an outburst like the one Gran had had the day before, she'd be drained and emotionally exhausted. Others would come and go with barely a ripple of effect.

Laney found Gran in the apartment's tiny kitchen. Though the kitchenette was spartan, it did have a coffeemaker. And Gran was pouring herself a cup of decaf.

"I suppose you'd like a cup?" Gran asked, her tone edged with annoyance.

It almost made her smile. Gran's best days—the days she was most like herself—always started with that same sharp tone. "No thanks. I stopped on the way." She gestured with her Einstein Brothers Bagels mug.

"Well, you might as well have some." Gran gave a beleaguered sigh. "I've already brewed it."

Now this was the grandmother Laney knew—all gruff annoyance and rough edges.

Laney crossed to the coffeepot as Gran lowered herself to one of the two chairs at the tiny table. She made a show of topping off her coffee even though Gran brewed it too weak for Laney's taste.

"You seemed to be feeling well," Laney said conversationally as she stirred in the few granules of sugar she added.

"Of course I am. You know how I am. As healthy as any-one who's…" But then she broke off, frowning.

"Eighty-three," Laney quickly supplied.

"I know how old I am," Gran grumbled, though Laney could see that she hadn't known. The age, which should have been on the tip of her tongue, hadn't been anywhere near the surface of her memory. A thing like that could turn a good day bad.

So Laney quickly changed the subject. "You have your checkup tomorrow. I've written it on the calendar, but I wanted to remind you. I'll be by first thing."

Gran took a sip of her coffee, staring at Laney from over her mug. "You're seeing someone new, aren't you?"

Laney paused midstir and then slowly pulled the spoon from the mug. "Why do you say that?"

Gran snorted. "After eighteen years of watching you make a fool of yourself over men, I think I know the signs."

Laney resisted the urge to throw the spoon in the sink. In-stead, she carefully hand washed it, towel dried it and returned it to the silverware drawer. Matilda's mind may be slippery, but the woman could still do her math.

The spoon-washing exercise gave Laney the chance to swallow the smart-ass reply she wanted to make. Funny thing was, the stress of dealing with Gran's really bad days didn't get to Laney. It was the good days that wore her down. Those were the days they grated on each other's nerves. The good days made it easy to fall into the same old patterns of an-tagonism.

"You're mistaken, Grandmother. I'm not seeing anyone."

"Fine. You don't have to tell me anything. You always were so closed off. Even as a little girl."

Laney didn't point out that she hadn't been closed off when she'd first come to live with Gran. She'd been grieving for her father. By the time she'd regained her emotional footing, she'd learned that Gran wasn't the kind to hand out hugs and cuddles.

"I'm not seeing anyone," she repeated. And she wasn't, was she?

Gran ignored her. "Well, I just hope it's not that man you had here with you yesterday."

Laney jerked her head up to look at Matilda. "Yesterday?"

Gran blew out an exasperated sigh. "Yes. Yesterday."

"I didn't know... You remember him?"

"Of course I remember him. Why wouldn't I?" And then, as if she didn't want an answer to that question, she kept talking without giving Laney a chance to answer. "I didn't like the look of him. He looked mean around the eyes." Her voice drifted off. "He reminded me of someone."

Himself probably...

Laney had no idea how to respond to Matilda's words. Laney didn't want to say anything that would set Gran off.

Gran frowned, her brain struggling to piece something together. After a moment, her hand snaked across the table and she grabbed Laney's hand. "You stay away from him. He'll crush you, Vee. I know what he's capable of. I know you think you love him, but he's a monster."

Laney hid her cringe as Gran's nails dug into her. There it was again—the name Vee. Yesterday, Gran had been so frantic, Laney had thought she'd misheard, but obviously not, because Gran had called her that again. She used her free hand to stroke the back of Matilda's hand until her muscles relaxed their death grip. "I'll stay away from him. I'm not going to let him hurt me."

"You be safe, Laney." Gran's voice was softer now, and when she said Laney's name, her tone oozed love in a way it never did when she was fully herself.

"I'll be safe," she promised, and finally Gran released her grip. Laney continued to stroke Matilda's fragile hand, her skin papery thin beneath Laney's fingers. "I'm not going to let him hurt me."

She didn't even flinch as she made the promise. She'd spent her entire adult life staying ahead of emotional commitments and the pain they caused. Not getting hurt was her specialty.

Eight

Even though Dalton was desperate to see Laney again, he never dreamed he'd see her so soon or that she'd be the one to contact him. Or that she'd come to Cain Enterprises.

She'd shown up Monday just before lunch.

He was on a conference call with the Midland office when an instant message from his assistant, Sydney, popped up on his computer, telling him that Laney had stopped by. He ended the call as quickly as possible, and five minutes from the time he got the message, Laney was strolling into his office carrying two bags of take-out food.

"I brought lunch," she announced, bursting into the room. Today she was dressed in denim shorts and a swishy blue tank top that was the exact color of ocean where the shallows dropped off. Everything about her, from the windblown look of her hair to the pink flush of her cheeks, reminded him of a perfect day spent out on the boat surrounded by nothing but the wind and water.

"I hope you don't mind vegetarian," she was saying. "I figured your schedule was busy, and I didn't want to take up too much of your workday." She must have read the surprise on his face, because she paused in the act of pulling out a take-out box. "You don't have lunch plans, do you? I should have asked first."

"I don't have lunch plans." In fact, he'd planned to send Sydney down to the on-site cafeteria to grab him something so he could eat while on the call with the Midland office. But since he was no longer taking that call, it was a moot point now.

He stood and rounded the desk to accept one of the take-out bags.

"I don't want to look gift takeout in the mouth, but shouldn't you be in school?"

"You can thank Columbus."

"Excuse me?"

"It's Columbus Day. You know, one of those holidays that most people don't pay much attention to but that teachers love because the state gives us a day off."

"I see."

"I figured this was the perfect time to get a jump-start on our case."

"*Our* case?" Perhaps he should have emphasized *case* rather than *our*. "We don't have a case."

"Of course we do." She gave an exaggerated *are you daft?* look. "It's the case of the missing heiress."

"Which is exactly what it would be titled if we were characters in a mystery novel. Which we're not. You're not Nancy Drew."

Laney winced. "Ooh, I hope not. Way too Goody Two-shoes. I'm more of a Veronica Mars type." Laney plucked herself down on the edge of his desk, so her butt was about three inches away from his in-box.

He forcibly dragged his gaze away from her enticing curves and tried to follow the conversation. "Veronica...what?"

"Veronica Mars. Plucky girl detective? The show wasn't

on for long, but it's developed a cult following? Not familiar at all, is it?" She smiled, like she knew exactly what he was thinking. "You really don't watch much TV, do you?"

"No." He pushed back his chair and stood. "Stop trying to distract me. This isn't a case. And it's certainly not something you're working on."

With her sitting on the desk and him standing, he had nearly a foot of height on her. Besides which, he'd been told—more than once—that he was an imposing man. *Grim* and *dour* were the words Portia most often used. While it wasn't an image he cultivated, he did occasionally use it to his advantage. But if he was so imposing, then it sure would have been nice if Laney would respond appropriately and cower before him in intimidation. But then, Laney never had been normal, had she?

"Since Columbus Day is your day off, you should go home and relax."

She grinned up at him. "I can think of a lot of things I could do at home, but on Saturday you were the one in favor of waiting, remember?"

One of her feet dangled near his leg. She wore a pair of sparkly flip-flops. She let one of them drop to the ground and then ran her toe along the outside of his calf, just in case her meaning wasn't clear.

It was.

Even through the fabric of his pants, he felt the warmth of her touch, and it drove him crazy—not merely the touch but the easy informality of it.

Between Saturday and today, she'd ratcheted her brazen sensuality up to stun. It was a reaction he remembered all too well from their high-school days. This wasn't a come-on, it was a defensive mechanism.

And he wasn't even sure he could blame her. She was so scared of letting him close that she was doing her damnedest to push him. The fact that she was willing to come here to

Cain Enterprises—the veritable lion's den—to see him was an indication of how desperate she was.

He didn't want her brazen. He didn't want her scared or bristly. He wanted to peel back the many layers of her defenses to the Laney she hid beneath. The real Laney. But he knew he'd never get the chance if he gave in and slept with her now. And he'd never do it here at Cain Enterprises either.

He stepped away, removing himself from the temptation of touching her. If he was going to eat with her, he needed to do it with at least a conference table between them—and possibly a force field.

Yes, he wanted her—of course he did—but he wanted more from her than the quickie she'd been offering up yesterday.

He nodded toward the door to the executive conference room. "Let's eat in there. There's more room." Maybe then he could shake the image of her ass on his desk out of his mind. As he swung open the door, he said, "As for the heiress, I don't want you getting involved with this."

She grabbed the two bags of takeout and followed. "Too late. You're the one who came to me, remember?"

"Yeah, I came to you so that you'd give me access to your grandmother. Not so you could play the plucky girl detective."

She dropped an enormous purse on the floor and then set the take-out bags on the conference table and quickly unloaded them, popping open one of the boxes to reveal edamame.

"It's as simple as this. I can help. Matilda can help. I just have to figure out how to ask the right questions. And obviously ask them without you there so that she won't freak out again."

Not for the first time, he wondered if Matilda really had information he could use. Had he ever really believed she might, or had he started on this path because he knew it would eventually lead him back to Laney? Was he really trying to find his father's missing daughter, or was he just lying to himself?

"Maybe your grandmother doesn't know anything," he said gently to Laney.

"Maybe you're right." She picked one of the edamame pods from the box and ran her finger along the edge, prying it open. "Maybe she knows nothing. But there's no harm in digging a little deeper."

She popped three edamame beans into her mouth and then cast aside the empty shell.

"It's not your job to do. It's mine. And I'm not supposed to have any outside help."

"Your father set up this stupid challenge, and you can't even get help? He said that?"

"I can't hire a detective. Plucky or not."

"Well, then, since I don't have a P.I. license, I think we're safe." She reached into her enormous purse and pulled out a spiral notebook with a white cartoon cat on the front. "I've started making a list of—"

"Why are you doing this?"

She looked up from her notebook, frowning.

"Two days ago, you were actively trying to get in my way. Now, all of a sudden, you're playing Veronica…"

"Mars," she supplied. With a sigh, she flipped open the notebook. "Come on, let me help you. Please?"

He watched her for a moment, pretending to consider her request for longer than he actually did. The truth was he couldn't deny her anything, but that wasn't exactly the kind of thing he wanted her to know either. No woman had ever had him eating out of the palm of her hand—at least not until Laney had walked back into his life.

She arched an eyebrow. "You have any better leads?"

"No," he admitted. "I don't." In fact, he was fresh out of ideas. He'd been back to visit his father twice in the past week. Both times, he'd left emotionally exhausted. Hollister claimed he wanted them to find this missing daughter of his, and yet he wasn't very forthcoming with details that might help Dalton find the girl. Dalton was left wondering: Did Hollister really care if she was found or was he just playing King Lear? Was he just testing their devotion with this pointless quest? It was a question Dalton couldn't consider right now, so he pushed it aside.

"I've been trying to narrow down the time frame. Just to give me somewhere to start. My father swears that he was faithful to my mother for the first four years of their marriage."

"Wow, what a saint," Laney muttered, as she pulled the notebook back to her and found a clean page. "So that means we can eliminate from…"

"June of 1978 to November of 1982."

"What's 1982?"

"That's when he met Cooper's mother in Switzerland."

"Ah." She jotted that down. "Great. That leaves us…what? Sixty-three years of his life to research. Awesome."

Dalton chuckled despite himself. "I think we can probably also knock out at least the first fifteen years of life. I can't guarantee that he wasn't pissing people off when he was a kid, but he probably wasn't seducing women and abandoning them that young."

"Good point." Laney did some math on the corner of the page and wrote down a few more dates. "That leaves us with a window of time from 1961 to 1978 and from 1982 until now." She gave an impressed whistle. "Boy, your father is quite the jerk."

"You don't know the half of it. On the bright side, the letter used the phrase 'years ago,' so we can probably rule out the last decade or so. That narrows our search a little."

She pushed her chair back, pulling one of her feet up onto the seat and wrapping her arm around her knee. "Tell me something. Why do you do it?"

"Excuse me?"

"Why do you put up with it? With the way he treats you. All of you."

"I do it because this is my company too."

"I did some research on you and—"

"You researched me?" A smile broke out across his face—one he couldn't contain.

She looked chagrined. "Yeah, yeah. Consider your ego stroked."

"No, seriously," he interrupted before she could brush him off again. "Why research me?"

She didn't quite meet his gaze. Instead, she grabbed another edamame pod from the take-out box and slit it open with her thumbnail.

Watching Laney eat was as erotic as a peep show. It made him think of all kinds of things she could do with her mouth and those long, slender fingers of hers. It was distracting enough he almost forgot the question he had asked.

"We've known each other for years," he said gently. "It seems like you'd know everything you needed to know about me."

Her shoulders gave a fidgety shift as she reached for another pod. "The Dalton I knew was a kid. I wanted to find out what kind of man you'd grown into." Finally her eyes moved back to his. "You asked for a lot of trust right out of the gate, Dalton. You wanted to see Gran. You promised to give money to the Woodland Theater. I…" She gave another evasive shrug. "It seemed like the smart move."

"You researched me because you didn't trust me." He sank back against his chair, feeling strangely defeated.

"Would you have trusted you? With the history between us?"

He blew out a breath. She was right, of course. He'd turned his back on her when she'd needed a friend. Only a fool would blindly trust someone who'd done that. "What did you find out?"

She gave him a long look, as if maybe she heard the resignation in his voice. Then she spoke, slowly reciting what she'd learned. "You're the model of the modern executive. Since you took over Cain Enterprises five years ago, the company has made *Fortune*'s '100 Best Companies to Work For' list three years running. *Men's Health* did an article on your innovations in fitness in the workplace. And you've managed to increase profits."

"You found out all that?"

"God bless Google." She tapped the edges of her notebook to even them out. "But here's what I don't get. You're clearly successful."

"The shareholders think so."

"In your own right. You've got an MBA from Wharton. You're well educated. You're intelligent. Plus, you have Cain Enterprises' most recent successes under your belt. You don't have to put up with Hollister's abuse. You could walk away. Go work somewhere else. Cain Enterprises isn't the only billion-dollar company that needs a CEO."

"Yeah," he said drily. "I may have to."

She frowned, because his answer was clearly not what she was expecting. "*Have* to?"

"If I don't find the missing heiress, I don't get Cain Enterprises."

"What?"

"I thought I told you on the first day. If I don't find her, I lose everything."

"Yeah, you said that. I just thought you were being…metaphorical or something."

"Nope. Whoever finds the heiress gets the company. If Hollister dies before anyone finds her, the company reverts to the state."

Laney sank back against the chair, suddenly looking pale. "You're kidding?" Then she shook her head. "Forget I said that. I know you'd never kid about that." Then she hopped out of her chair and paced for a few steps before whirling back to him. "So that's it? If you don't find this heiress, you lose everything?"

"Not everything. I have my own money. Stock options from my years of working for Cain myself. My education." He flashed a self-deprecating smile. "My charm."

She snorted. "Well, at least you won't be living in a cardboard box on the streets. But still. This is proof. Hollister is psychotic. You know that, right?"

"Yeah. That's a theory I've been working on for years."

"The bastard!" She continued to pace, clenching and un-clenching her hand as she rounded the table.

Despite the grim conversation, he nearly laughed at Laney's violent indignation on his behalf. How long had it been since he'd had anyone so firmly in his corner? Years...probably since they were kids.

It made him smile seeing Laney in full-on warrior mode. It reminded him all too well of the girl she's been in high school—full of piss and vinegar and always just one piercing away from looking like an extra from *Sid and Nancy*.

"You know what I think you should do?" she asked suddenly. "I think you should tell him to go to hell."

"Of course you do." She hadn't changed that much since high school after all.

"You can't let him hold you over a barrel like this. You should just quit now."

"I'm not going to quit," he said simply.

"Why not? Your father's an ass. You're a well-respected businessman. There are probably dozens of other companies that would hire you. Hell, go start your own company."

"You're right. I could do all of that. But then I wouldn't have Cain Enterprises."

"And Cain Enterprises is so damn important to you?"

"Yes. It is. You don't understand the sacrifices I've made to be the CEO."

"Then explain it."

"This is what I was raised to do. I've known I was the heir to the company for as long as I can remember. I knew it was mine, but it's always been mine to lose. Hollister made it clear that if I messed up I'd lose everything."

He paused and reflected for a moment. "I was seven the first time Hollister brought Cooper home with him for the summer."

"That must have made for a fun summer break."

"You have no idea. Mother was pissed as hell. Livid. Lines were drawn."

"You had to choose between your mother and your father, and you picked your father's side." Laney's tone was flat. And she didn't ask it like a question. She didn't have to. By the time she'd moved into the carriage-house apartment, the lines that had been drawn that long ago summer were as deep and as broad as a World War I no-man's-land.

"I didn't think of it as picking my father's side. I picked the side with my future on it. I've used that same criterion for every decision I've made since then. Every time I picked a class or a sport or a school or a girlfriend, I thought, 'Will this make me a better leader? Will this help me run Cain Enterprises?'"

"Not every decision." Again her voice was quiet, and he almost got the sense that she hadn't meant to say it aloud.

"No, not every decision," he agreed, because he knew she was probably thinking about the summer she came to live in the carriage house.

Befriending the scrawny, rebellious granddaughter of his housekeeper hadn't benefited him in any way. But he'd done it anyway. Something in her spirit had spoken to him even then, and he'd been unable to resist her.

When he'd befriended her at the age of thirteen, the decision hadn't seemed like a big deal, but cutting her out of his life at sixteen had taken monumental strength of will. He hadn't wanted to lose her. He wouldn't have done it unless he was absolutely certain that it was best for both of them. She couldn't possibly realize how that decision had cost him. "After all the sacrifices I've made, I've given up too much for this company. There's no way I'm letting it go now."

Nine

Listening to him talk, Laney felt like her heart might break. Had she ever had anyone who loved her the way he loved Cain Enterprises? She wasn't sure what made her sadder—the fact that he felt that way about a company and not about her, or the fact that he might lose it all. Laney forced a bright smile. "Well, wasn't that just the most joyful conversation ever?"

Surprise flickered across Dalton's face, and then he laughed, looking embarrassed. "Yeah. Just about." Then he sank back into his chair. "Sorry."

"No, don't apologize."

"I should be able to talk about this without sounding like a psychotic lunatic."

"You didn't sound psychotic. Just very, very passionate." She was quiet for a moment and then added, "Everyone needs something they're passionate about. You're lucky that you found your something so young."

He smiled, as though maybe he agreed. But then he gave his

head a shake as he turned back to the table. "No, I'm lucky if I find this missing girl. I'll be lucky if I don't lose everything."

Laney bit down hard on an edamame bean, ignoring the way her teeth clattered together. She didn't like that word: everything...not the way he used it anyway.

Yeah, sure, she knew this going in. Cain Enterprises was everything to Dalton. She was thankful he'd reminded her of where she stood in his life, reminded her that this—whatever this was between them—was temporary. An itch to scratch and nothing more. As long as she remembered that and kept her emotions out of this, she'd be fine. She'd have to be.

"While we're on the subject of that sword hanging over your head, let me fill you in on what I found out."

"You found out something?"

"Well, it's not so much found out as remembered." She flipped a few pages back in her notebook and tapped the eraser of her pencil against the page. "I've been thinking about what Matilda said when she saw you."

"When she lost it and we had to call the orderlies to come sedate her?"

"Yeah, I know what you're thinking."

"I'm thinking I'm glad I wasn't pinning all my hopes on your skills as a detective."

She fluttered her eyelashes at him. "Are you teasing me, Mr. Cain? Because that's awfully cruel of you when you haven't even heard me out."

"Okay, then. Impress me."

"You're thinking she was just stringing together rambling nonsense, which is what I thought at first too. But then when I went back yesterday, she mentioned you and—"

"She mentioned me?"

"Well, not you precisely. She didn't call you by name. She mentioned the man who'd come to visit the day before. Meaning you. And then she said—" she peered down at the notebook and read from the page "—'Stay away from him. He'll crush you, Vee. I know what he can do. You love him, but he's a monster.' I wrote it down as soon as I left."

"And?"

"And, she called me Vee. I may not have gotten it word for word, but I know she called me Vee, which she also did on Saturday when you were there."

"Yeah. I know. I just assumed that was something she called you sometimes."

"No, she's never called me that before. And she's never been so upset that she didn't seem to recognize me."

"She also called you Elaine."

She waved aside his argument. "I know, but that's normal. I mean, sometimes she seems to think I'm her sister. She calls me Elaine. She's been doing that for years."

"But she's never called you anything else before? Other than Laney or Elaine?"

"Sometimes, she seems to think I'm my mother. She calls me Suzy-Q."

"That's sweet."

"Not the way she says it. She hated my mother. But that's it. It's either Laney, Elaine or Suzy-Q. She was diagnosed in 2008. She started mixing up the names a few years before that. In all this time, she's never called me Vee. Or even mentioned a Vee."

"Are you sure it's even a name?"

"You're awfully skeptical for a man with few other leads."

"I'd be less skeptical if we had more to go on than a name she happened to mention while I was there." His tone implied he thought she was wasting her time.

"Just hear me out, okay? This Vee woman, whoever she is, is someone my grandmother felt protective about. My grandmother worried about her."

"Your point?"

"This is my grandmother. You remember what she's like, right? She was a battle-ax but with fewer soft edges. My grandmother prided herself on her efficiency, her organization and her cooking, not her people skills. She wasn't a nurturing person, and she wasn't a worrywart. If she worried about this woman, it's because she was genuinely afraid for her."

"Okay. I'll buy that. But that doesn't mean it has anything to do with my father."

"Right." She turned the page again and pushed the notebook across the table to him. "I thought of that too. So the first thing I did was go online and research my family to see if there were daughters with that name."

"And…"

"None. No V names at all, unless I go all the way back to Vernon Pratter, a distant cousin born in 1896."

"Unlikely."

"Right. I don't want to oversimplify things. But what if Vee worked for your parents?"

"You jump from Vee isn't anyone in your family to maybe she worked for my parents? That's a pretty big leap. Vee—assuming she's even a person—could be anyone. She could be a friend from school, next-door neighbor growing up, the checkout girl from the grocery store."

Laney rolled her eyes. "Now you're just being difficult. Gran never had a lot of friends. She was close to our family and yours. When Gran thought she was talking to Vee, she sounded really worried. She cared about her. And whoever Vee is, she's someone Matilda thought of in association with Hollister."

Dalton seemed to be considering it, but even if she couldn't convince him completely, she knew she was right. Call it gut instinct, call it a hunch…whatever. She knew she was right.

"Look, it's worth looking into. When you three boys were younger, your parents hired all kinds of extra help, right?"

"Sure, there were nannies and groundskeepers. But only your grandmother stayed on after we grew up."

"Do you remember any of the nannies?"

Dalton was quiet, and for a minute, she thought he was going to dismiss her idea again, but then he said, "There was a Julie when Griffin was young. And Rachel after that. She was the last, I think. And, um…maybe a Sophia. That's it."

"Oh." She blew out a breath, disappointed.

"That's it as in that's all I can remember. There were more than just those three—a lot more. I just don't remember their names."

"Can you find them out?"

"I think we better."

There was a note of finality and determination in his voice. Laney leaped up and clapped her hands. "You'll do it?"

"I have to. I don't have a lot else to go on. I've had Sydney scouring county records looking for any birth certificates that list Hollister as a father, but so far, we've come up with nothing. And considering we have no idea where this girl was born, or even if the mother listed Hollister at all, it's a long shot. This is the first lead we've found."

She smiled. "Look at you, talking like a detective already."

And using the word *we,* but she didn't say that part aloud—she had to maintain some dignity around him.

She tried not to beam with satisfaction as he called his assistant in and asked the woman to look up the employment records of anyone who'd worked for the family in the past forty years.

Laney might have been jealous of Dalton's pretty young assistant, but the woman was so cool and professional, Laney couldn't imagine her having a relationship with anyone, let alone her boss.

By the time Sydney left, Laney was frowning again, though. "Do you think she'll be able to find anything? Forty years is a long time."

"I certainly hope so. Your grandmother kept the household records the entire time she worked there, and as you pointed out yourself, she was efficient. I'm sure she kept track of everyone who worked there. If not, there's always tax records."

"I thought the rule on personal taxes was that you were

supposed to keep them for three years, seven if you're doing something illegal. Not forty."

Dalton's mouth stretched into a predatory smile. "Well, then, let's hope my parents were doing something very illegal."

She nearly laughed at the ferocity in his gaze but didn't want him to take it the wrong way. The truth was that it was fun being on the same side of the fight with him. And, yeah, she'd relished antagonizing him in high school. But this? This was *way* more fun.

Shaking her head, she said, "Something tells me your parents might be in serious trouble."

"You don't approve?"

"Of you digging around in your parents' past?" She shrugged. "Hey, your dad is the one who started all this. I say, have at it. I just don't know whether I should try to rein you in or pop popcorn and settle in for a good show."

The lines of his smile softened with genuine humor. He leaned back in his chair then, kicking it back onto two legs with effortless arrogance. His gaze raked over her, and she felt the intensity of it all the way down to her very bones. She shivered, feeling inexplicably like their relationship was shifting yet again.

Then abruptly, he dropped the legs of the chair back to the ground and glanced at his watch. He stood, saying, "I have an appointment this afternoon. If you'll ride along with me, we can keep talking on the way."

Some part of her wanted to jump at the chance—the same part that had to resist beaming when he agreed with her. The part that filled with girlish joy every time he smiled at her. Which was ridiculous, because she wasn't one of those silly, girlish types. Even when she'd been a girl, she hadn't acted like that. As a kid, she'd gone straight from *Sesame Street* to tree climbing to chipped black nail polish, with nary a glass slipper or pink tutu in between. But now, around Dalton— Dalton of all people—she felt giggly and girlish. It was as exhilarating as it was terrifying.

She was still weighing the pros and cons—the pro being the chance to spend more time with him, the con being the ever-increasing risk of having her heart smushed into tiny bits—when Dalton said, "I'd like for you to come."

Oh, God, how was she supposed to say no to that?

"The food…" she protested weakly.

"We'll bring it with us." He closed the top to one of the take-out boxes and put it back in the bag.

Before she could protest, the food was all packed up and she was walking out to his car. The ease with which he convinced her to come with him didn't bode well for all those tiny bits of her heart. She had no illusions about their future. Whatever this spark was between them, she had to make sure it was only physical. Not emotional. She was supposed to be keeping him away from Gran and keeping him away from her heart. She could do that, right? She was tough. She always had been. And if worse came to worst, she'd just have to hope that falling out of all those trees had prepared her heart for a much greater fall.

She wondered later if her time wouldn't have been better spent preparing not for heartache but for surprise.

For starters, Dalton didn't spend the drive discussing leads or theories or anything related to the missing Cain heiress or anything related to Cain Enterprises. Instead, he asked her question after question about her years since high school. At first she answered only briefly, but gradually—as it became more evident that the drive wasn't a short one—her answers filled out. She found herself talking about the year off she'd taken between high school and college—a year that had turned into three, during which she'd traveled, first in the United States and then in Europe. She told him how she'd spent ten months in Italy learning to speak the language, visiting all the museums, struggling to accept the fact that she did not have her grandmother's gift in the kitchen and eventually finding the village where her great-grandfather had lived before emigrating to the United States.

By the time she realized she'd been doing all the talking, they'd been in the car nearly an hour. Also, they were no longer in Houston proper but had reached one of the harbors in the bay area.

"You have an appointment on a boat?" she asked as Dalton stopped the car at a security gate to swipe a clearance badge.

The gate opened, allowing him to drive past. "Did I say I had an appointment?"

"Yes." A pristine green park dotted with cypress trees gave way to dozens of boat slips and the murky gray waters of Galveston Bay beyond. "You said you had an appointment this afternoon."

Dalton maneuvered the car past row after row of boats and sailboats, their bare masts bobbing against the clear blue sky. His express was serious, but she could see the hint of a smile tugging at his lips. "I thought I just said I had plans."

"No. You used the word *appointment.* I'm sure of it."

"Well, then, I'm sorry I misled you." He pulled the car into a parking spot near a dock on a far end of the marina and killed the engine.

"Lured me is more like it," she grumbled.

He turned toward her, draping his arm over the steering wheel. "It's a gorgeous afternoon. A great day to be out on the water. You have the day off anyway. Why not spend it on my boat?"

Why not indeed? After all, she was the one who'd been pushing to tip their relationship over the edge. But an afternoon on a boat? That seemed so…picturesque. So romantic. So very much like something out of those romantic comedies she tried so hard to hate.

"Did it ever occur to you to just ask me before driving me all the way out here?"

"Of course it did. And then it occurred to me that you'd probably say no and then list a slew of more practical ways you planned to spend the day—none of which would be the real reason you didn't want to come."

Her breath hitched. "And I suppose you think you know the real reason I would have said no?"

"Of course I do. You don't want to be alone with me."

She wanted to argue with that, but he was completely right. Plus it seemed like sacrilege to lie when staring out at such a gorgeous view.

He reached across and brushed a knuckle down her cheek. She nearly jumped at his touch. "Look, you can relax, Laney. I promise I didn't bring you out here to seduce you."

Yeah, but it was the *not seducing her* that was killing her.

"Let's just enjoy the day. Besides, if I lose everything, the million-dollar boat will be the first thing to go. If I don't take her out now, who knows when I'll get the chance to take her out again?"

It was all Laney could do not to snort in disbelief. "You spent a million dollars on a boat?"

He flashed her a chastened look. "Technically, my father spent a million on the boat. He was going to sell her earlier this year, and I bought her from him."

"Oh, well, that's much better," she muttered, before clicking her seat belt off and climbing out of the car. "Okay, let's see what a million bucks buys in a boat."

He caught up with her at the nose of the car, and together they headed down the dock.

Dalton glanced at her. "Is this a good time to mention that this technically isn't a boat?"

"Well, it's not a hippopotamus, that's for sure."

"It's a yacht."

"Jeez." She rolled her eyes, walking a few steps before asking, "Is this a good time to tell you that—technically—I can't swim?"

Dalton jerked to a stop. "Seriously?"

She turned back to see that Dalton had gone white. She

couldn't quite tell if it was shock or fear on his face. Either way she had to chuckle. "Of course not. I was joking."

"Are you sure? Because we don't have to go out on the boat."

"Yes, I'm sure. I was just teasing. Jeez, you take everything this seriously?"

But she didn't need him to answer the question, because she knew that, yes, Dalton Cain did take everything this seriously. He'd been like that as a boy too—so solemn and quiet. She'd been eleven when she'd first gone to live in the Cains' carriage house. In terms of age, she was neatly sandwiched between Dalton and Griffin and Cooper. With Griffin and Cooper, she'd climbed trees and played tag football. They'd built forts in the backyard and gone on hikes through the wet-weather creeks behind the Cain property.

She'd done none of those things with Dalton. With him, she'd learned to play chess and listened to music, not just the gritty grunge that she already liked at eleven but to musicians he loved, such as Yo-Yo Ma and Count Basie and David Brubeck—music she still listened to. He'd taken her on a walking tour of the Cain mansion—that was his word: walking tour—and showed all the artwork in the house, telling her about the artist, the period, the style. He even told her which were fakes and which were real, because even rich people owned fakes since almost no one knew all the lesser paintings of the masters.

To her eleven-year-old self, Dalton had been a fascinating mystery—so complex and bizarre and unlike any other boy she'd ever known. So completely different from her world of Top 40 music and McDonald's and lazy summers watching the *Power Rangers*. She'd wondered at the time why he bothered with her at all.

Now, walking down the dock to his boat—scratch that, his yacht—she remembered all these things about him. Memories that she'd somehow ruthlessly shoved aside until now, things she buried deep inside her soul. Because Dalton had partly made her who she was. He'd stirred her curiosity and her ambition in a way no one had before or since.

Once their friendship ended in high school, she'd made herself forget all the wonderful times they'd had early in their friendship. She hadn't had room for those memories in her bruised heart. But now, looking back, she could enjoy reminiscing. She could welcome back the boy he'd been as well as enjoy the man he'd become.

Viewing their early relationship through the eyes of an adult, she could see now what she couldn't then. Instead of automatically pushing him away in anger, instead of trying to piss him off to get his attention, she should have talked to him. She should have tried to understand his point of view.

But the truth was, when he'd booted her out of his life a few years later, she'd been furious and hurt but not really surprised. She'd never understood why he'd bothered with her in the first place. He was worlds smarter and better educated than she was. She hadn't seen what she'd brought to the friendship.

Now, all these years later, she did. At eleven, she hadn't taken him nearly as seriously as he took himself. She hadn't yet understood that he was the heir to an empire. That he was more important than he seemed to be. She'd just wanted a friend. She'd probably been the only person in his life who'd ever wanted to be with him just because she enjoyed his company. She was the only person who teased him, the only person who dared anger him. Suddenly, she could see that he'd needed her just as desperately as she'd needed him.

She could also see that he needed her still—not forever but for today. Hollister's ridiculous demand had thrown Dalton's life into turmoil. Dalton needed a friend. He needed—just for now—someone who teased him and reminded him that life didn't have to be so serious. It could be fun too.

No wonder he'd lured her out here to the boat. This afternoon, he didn't need a plucky girl detective to help him find the missing heiress. He needed a playmate.

So when they reached the boat, she cocked her hip to the

side and propped her hand on it. "What, no gangplank? No captain to welcome me aboard?"

A smile teased at Dalton's lips, as if he saw right through her. "Nope," he said. "No captain. Just you, me and the water." He paused, looking at her. "You okay with that?"

There was enough heat in his gaze to simmer Galveston Bay.

Of course, the big flaw in her plan to give Dalton the afternoon off to play with a friend was that she wasn't sure they could be just friends. But maybe that wasn't a bad thing.

Could she spend the day with Dalton, being his friend *and* his lover? Could she let them both have just this one afternoon and then walk away tomorrow?

Yeah, she thought she could. She was good at walking away.

So she grinned and said, "Hey, I've been waiting to get you all alone for days."

Dalton's smile widened to a grin as he stepped nimbly from the dock onto the stern of the boat where it was only a few feet away from the edge of the dock. Without waiting to see if she followed, he went up a few steps to the top deck and disappeared for a moment. He moved with such easy grace it was obvious he'd been around boats all his life. She, on the other hand, had taken the ferry from Galveston to Bolívar a couple of times.

If she were honest with herself, she'd have to admit that Dalton intimidated her. Not the money or the yacht or even his position of power within Cain Enterprises. Those were all things he'd been born to. No, what most impressed her about Dalton was what he'd done with what he'd been given. The way his leadership had taken Cain Enterprises to the next level. The way he'd abandoned his father's business tactics in favor of his own.

He was an amazing man. How on earth had she ended up here with him?

It was a question she didn't dare ask herself. Not when it was so much easier to just enjoy the day and pretend he wouldn't break her heart when this ended.

Dalton disappeared briefly down a ladder into the cabin.

When he reappeared on the upper deck of the boat, he was barefoot and holding one of those key chains with the little floaty attached to the end. He almost looked ready to take off without her. She cleared her throat, and he looked up.

He came back down to the lower deck, rested an elbow on a stretch of railing and looked at her, eyebrow arched—again with that aren't-you-cute expression.

She looked pointedly from the boat to her spot on the deck. "You're going to make me say it, aren't you?"

His smile broadened. "You need help, right?"

"I would think that's rather obvious."

"Sometimes, asking for what you need is good for the soul."

She gave him a squinting-eyed look of feigned annoyance. "I asked you for a hundred grand. I think my soul's in good shape."

"No, you asked for a hundred grand for a bunch of kids. It's not the same thing."

"Okay, then." She blew out a breath and shot him a sassy smile. "Hey, Dalton, I don't know how to get on the boat— excuse me, the yacht. Will you please help me?"

"Sure." He pushed off with his shoulder and crossed the deck toward her as a boat in the channel zipped past Dalton's slip. He braced one hand on the railing and stretched his other out to her. "Just take my hand and step aboard."

As he said it, the wake from the other boat rocked his. Even the dock where she stood seemed to wobble beneath her feet. She placed her hand in his. "If I stumble, you have to catch me."

"I promise."

The boat swayed as she stepped across, and she ended up plastered against Dalton's body. Looking up into his eyes, Laney felt like she couldn't even pull air into her lungs. Maybe that was why her voice came out all low and breathless. "Thanks. Do you think I'll get my sea legs soon, or will I always be this wobbly?"

"Are you saying being near me made the earth move?"

"Ha-ha." She gave his chest a little shove, and he playfully stumbled back. "That boat was clearly going too fast."

He chuckled. "I'll alert the coast guard." Holding her elbow, he guided her over to the railing, making sure she had a hand-hold before releasing her. "You good now?"

She paused for a minute, feeling the gentle roll and pitch of the boat beneath her feet before she nodded. "I think so." She started up the stairs and then paused. "Hey, don't I need a life jacket or something?"

"Are you just procrastinating now?"

She gave his arm a playful sock. "No. I'm serious. Aren't I supposed to have a life vest on at all times?"

"Absolutely." He nodded seriously. "If you're thirteen or under."

"You laugh now, but I saw *Titanic*. If there aren't enough life jackets, it could be bad."

He chuckled out loud at that. "I'll try to avoid any icebergs floating in Galveston Bay. But if it makes you feel better, there are life jackets and an inflatable Zodiac boat under the benches. If the yacht goes down, you'll be fine."

"What about you?"

"If the yacht goes down, I'll be devastated."

He took her hand and guided her up the four steps to the upper deck. She didn't need help—not with the railing there—but since she'd made a fuss getting on the bo...on the yacht, she accepted his help and told herself it was good for her soul.

Most of this deck was dominated by a pair of L-shaped benches, one along the stern out in the open, the other along the port side and tucked up under the roof opposite the captain's chair. Interspersed between them were end tables, a mini fridge and a wet bar. The seating was done in supple white leather and the tables in sleek, polished wood. In the center, tucked under the windshield, was the ladder that led down to the cabin. Through the open doorway, she spied more leather, more gleaming chrome and more extravagant luxury.

If his car was understated, then his yacht most certainly was not. Stunning and impressive? Check. Bigger than her duplex and nearly long enough to park an eighteen-wheeler on top of? Check. Modest? Um, not so much.

There was no mistaking this for anything other than what it was: the plaything of a wealthy man.

Dalton gestured toward the seats at the stern of the boat. "You're welcome to sit wherever you want, but those seats can get a little warm in this sun. If you sit up here under the roof, you'll have shade. And I can open this window here so you'll still get a nice breeze." He slid open one of the port-side windows. "I could turn on the air conditioner, but it just seems silly."

"No thanks, I'm good."

"There are drinks in the fridge," he said as he pulled a pair of sunglasses from a compartment near the helm.

"You want something?" She hopped up. A quick check of the fridge revealed a selection of ice-cold beer, soda and wine, as well as trays of fruit and cheese. If she had to guess, the galley down the stairs was fully stocked as well. All of that seemed pretty normal. What unnerved her were the silver cans of Barq's root beer. She'd drunk Barq's when she was a kid. It had been her favorite drink when all the other girls were drinking Diet Coke. Did he remember that?

Obviously, someone at the marina had stocked the yacht before they'd arrived. Was this the standard service the marina provided? Or had he done all this just for her? Was he wooing her?

How was she supposed to maintain her defenses against him? She could handle the Dalton who was arrogant and obsessed with finding the heiress. That Dalton needed her only so he could maintain his hold on Cain Enterprises. But this guy? This guy who left work in the middle of the day to go boating? She wasn't sure what to do with this Dalton. This seemed like a guy who could win her heart as well as her body. And that terrified her, because she'd misled him about Gran. Once he knew the truth, he wouldn't want her heart or her body.

Then she felt Dalton's hand on her shoulder. "Hey, you don't get seasick do you?"

She turned to face him. "No. I mean, I don't think so. Why?"

"You didn't answer when I asked you to hand me a root

beer." He brushed her hair off her cheek and cupped her jaw. "And you look a little pale."

"You drink Barq's?" she asked. Then, as relief flooded her, she repeated. "*You* drink Barq's."

"Yeah," he said slowly, as if baffled by her confusion.

She nearly laughed then at her silliness. Here she was freaking out over soda, reading too much into the simplest things.

"No. I'm great. One Barq's coming up." She handed him a can, then moved some bottles around and extracted a Shiner beer from the back. She twisted the cap off and took a gulp, determined to put aside her paranoia for good and just enjoy the afternoon.

Then she sat, holding her beer in one hand and the armrest with the other as Dalton backed the yacht out of the slip and then maneuvered through the marina out into the bay. He should have looked absurd, since he'd come here straight from work and the attire of a CEO was hardly boat worthy. But somehow his tan pants and white linen shirt looked breezy and casual, now that he'd rolled up the sleeves on his shirt and lost his shoes.

Despite the fresh, salty air blowing in through the window, she found herself tugging at the neck of her tank top. It wasn't just his good looks that heated her blood. There was something else about him—some ineffable quality that she'd never quite been able to define. Maybe it was his intelligence. Maybe it was his confidence, which in a man who'd accomplished less in his life might be perceived as arrogance. Or maybe it was just the sheer tenacity of his focus.

Dalton had the unique ability to focus so intently on something that it seemed as if nothing else existed in the world. And right now, this afternoon, even though he was driving the boat, he was focusing on her.

It was a heady feeling, knowing that she had him all to herself from now until whenever he turned the boat around and they returned to civilization. But it was terrifying too.

She could handle being a rich man's plaything for an afternoon—just so long as that's all it was. But what if there was something more going on? What if he was playing for keeps?

Ten

It took nearly an hour just to get out of Galveston Bay, but once they'd passed Galveston he turned the boat northeast and headed up the coast to his favorite stretch near the McFaddin National Wildlife Refuge. Gradually, the coastal homes gave way to lush, green wetlands. The pelicans and seagulls that swarmed the bay gradually thinned out and were replaced by the more exotic birds of the refuge. Bitterns and egrets dotted the shoreline as white geese swooped low over the water in graceful flocks. Out here, on the ocean, with no one else around except other boats dotting the water in the distance and the seabirds or the occasional bottlenose dolphin, this was one of the few places he truly felt free to relax.

Normally, he felt his cares slip away as soon as he stepped onto the dock. Today was different—not nerves, not even tension. More…awareness.

Laney, he'd noticed, wasn't exactly at ease on his boat. Despite her claims that she knew how to swim, he wondered if maybe that wasn't the problem. However, Laney was the kind of woman who didn't back down from a challenge. If it had been a matter as simple as a fear of water, she'd have faced it head-on. No, this was something else. This was something personal. Her tension didn't let up on the open water, and so when he spotted his favorite little cove near the nature preserve, he slowed the boat to a stop, turned off the motor and dropped anchor there in the shallows.

Then he turned to Laney, propped himself against the boat's dash and raised his sunglasses. She'd kicked off her shoes at some point and had her feet tucked up on the bench. She'd twisted to drape one arm along the back of the seat so she could stare out the windshield at the open water. Now, she raised her own sunglasses to the top of her head and met his gaze.

She feigned calm so well, she looked the very picture of relaxation. If he didn't know her better, he'd think she did this every day—or posed as a model for boat catalogs at least.

But he could see how tightly she was reining herself in. See how hard she had to work to appear relaxed. Her toes tapped out a silent rhythm against the leather. The label of her empty beer bottle had been peeled off. While steering the boat, he'd watched from the corner of his eye as she'd shredded the paper into tiny strips and then balled it into a condensation-dampened mess.

Now, as he studied her, he wondered if he'd made a mistake bringing her out here. Back on the dock, he'd seen straight through her bravado. He was old friends with her bluster and bristle. He'd known, of course, that it hid some other emotion that she didn't want him to see. Some vulnerability that she kept close to her chest, which was where she kept everything she thought might make her appear weak.

He'd just assumed that whatever it was would fade away as they left the bay, as his cares always did, but maybe he'd been wrong. His assessments of people usually weren't, but Laney always defied his expectations in one way or another.

"You seem…" He hesitated as he chose the word. If Laney was feeling prickly he didn't want to make it worse. "On edge."

She gave an indelicate snort, which either could have meant he was stating the obvious or he was an idiot.

"You want me to head back?"

"No. I'm just confused about your motives for kidnapping me."

"Is that really how you see this? As a kidnapping?"

She shifted her feet back to the ground, keeping her legs pressed primly together, and crossed her arms over her chest. "You lured me out here. You didn't tell me where you were taking me. And now I'm God only knows how far from civilization with no idea what your motives were or when you're planning on taking me back."

"Well, when you put it that way, it does sound nefarious." He stepped to her and gently pulled one of her arms free before tugging her to her feet. Another step back and he was resting his backside against the console above the mini fridge and cradling her between his outstretched legs. "Will it help if I promise I'm not going to murder you and dump your body out at sea?"

She crossed her arms over her chest again, her mouth set in a pout. "It would help if I understood what your motives were."

"You know, some women would take a gesture like this at face value. They'd just enjoy the romantic afternoon at sea."

It was not that he wanted to be with any of those women. No, Laney, for all her prickliness and bluster, was the one he wanted.

She gave his chest a little shove. "So you admit it?"

"Admit what?" he asked, baffled.

"You bring a lot of women out here." She looked strangely cheered by the idea.

He chuckled. "Is that what's bothering you? You think I do this all the time?"

"You do, right? I mean, this is all straight out of the rich playboy seduction manual, right?"

There was something he couldn't read in her expression. If he took her words at face value, he'd say she sounded insecure. Like she was worried about being just one of his conquests. But surely she didn't really believe that? And the tone of her voice was all wrong. Like she *hoped* she was just a conquest.

Unsure what she wanted to hear, he said, "Tell me about this manual. Is this the manual for seducing playboys or the manual playboys use to seduce beguiling women?"

She gave his shoulder a little shove. "You know what I mean."

"What do you want me to say here? That I'm trying to impress you? That I wanted today to be special? The Barq's root beer was for you, because that's what you drank in high school. You also used to like wine coolers, but I took a leap of faith and guessed that maybe your taste had improved, so that's why there's a pinot grigio and a couple of bottles of red down in the galley. I texted the marina before we left Houston and had them take the boat out of storage, gas it up and stock it." He waited until her expression softened before adding, "I do not bring dates out on this boat. In fact, you're the first woman who's set foot on here since I bought her."

Laney frowned. "But your ex-wife—"

"Portia hated boats. And the Texas heat. Just not her thing. I didn't even buy the boat until after the divorce. You wouldn't know it by looking at her, but my mother loves being out on the water. I think she probably used the boat more than my father did when they owned it, but even she hasn't been out with me. When Hollister sold me this one, my mother picked out a little sailboat of her own."

Laney was quiet for a long moment as she stared, frowning, out the window, apparently sorting through what he'd told her.

He let her process his words but only for a minute before he asked, "Why is it so hard for you to believe?"

She gave another one of those snorts that he found so adorable and so confusing. "Well, believe it or not, this is the first time a handsome, rich guy has abducted me for the afternoon and taken me yachting."

"Yeah, I better be the first rich guy to abduct you for the afternoon."

She was so cutely petulant that he couldn't help pulling her closer and dropping a kiss on her mouth. Not a slow, lingering kiss—that would have gotten away from him too quickly—but a fast, possessive kiss. The kind he wanted to mark her with constantly.

When he lifted his head, her expression was so confused that he instantly wanted one of those slow, lingering kisses after all—the kind that would devour the rest of the afternoon and maybe even his whole soul.

He nudged her hips away from him, struggling to rein in his imagination, but he couldn't force himself to push her too far away. Not when he wanted her this badly.

She frowned up at him, her brow furrowed just a little. "Tell me something. Why?"

"Why what?"

"Why bring me out to the boat?"

"Is it so hard to believe I just wanted to spend the afternoon with you?"

"We were spending the afternoon together. At your office. Why bring me out here?"

Now he pushed her the rest of the way away from him, giving himself space to think and to pace. "No, we weren't spending the afternoon together at my office. We were grabbing a quick lunch while we talked about my father's manipulative bargain." Dalton bent down and snagged his own Shiner from the mini fridge, twisting the cap off with a vicious twist. "All the Cain employees were within shooting range, and I had three more meetings scheduled for later in the day. That's not spending the afternoon with you."

Laney just watched him, that same frown on her face. "So, what? You just wanted to play hooky because you're bored."

"This isn't boredom," he said, his own annoyance creeping into his voice. Damn it, why did she always have to be so damn difficult?

"Okay, then. Not bored." She waved a hand as if erasing the previous word. "Let's go with frustrated by your current lack of control in your own life. Angered by your father's edict. Pissed off that you're about to lose everything you've worked so hard for so you're venting your latent rebellion? Do any of those fit?"

"No." He slammed the beer down on the console and stalked over to her. "None of those fit. Because that's not what I'm feeling now. You can analyze me all you want, but if you're going to, get your facts right. This—" he gestured back and forth between them "—has nothing to do with my father or my latent rebelliousness or my lack of control or any of that."

Her scowl said she didn't believe him, so he kept talking.

"This is only about you and me. If I chose to take the afternoon off to play hooky with you, it's not about getting away from life, it's about being with you. Hell, do you have any idea how long I've wanted to do this?"

She mocked glancing at her watch. "Oh, about three hours? 'Cause I figure that's probably about when you called the marina."

"No. Figure about sixteen years."

Confusion flickered across her face. "What—"

"You and Eric Mulroney used to skip school on Friday afternoons."

She still had that look of baffled confusion. "We only went and hung out at the mall. Or sometimes at his house, if his parents weren't home. You…you could have come. Eric was your friend."

"Not after he started dating you, he wasn't." Dalton's words were full of anger and resentment. The force of them rocked her back, stunning her into silence.

She frowned, trying to remember. She'd met Eric because he was Dalton's friend. To be honest, that's why she'd dated him.

It had been her freshman year, the Friday after school had started. Dalton had ignored her all week. She'd known he was at home, because from her bedroom window, she could see the flickering of the TV screen in his room. Determined to find out why he was treating her so badly, she'd climbed the tree outside his window, shimmied across the branch and hopped into his bedroom, the way she had countless times over the past two years. She was shocked to find that he wasn't alone. He had a whole cadre of friends in his room, watching TV and playing video games, which was unusual for him.

"Well then, why did you introduce us?" she asked now.

"I had no choice. I had invited people over because I didn't want to have to talk to you. And then you came in through the damn window anyway. So I introduced you. And I knew the second Eric saw you that it was a mistake. I wanted—"

She raised her eyebrows, waiting for him to finish the sentence, suddenly desperate to know what that teenage Dalton had wanted on that long-ago afternoon. Because, even then, he'd kept his emotions tightly reined in.

"What?" she prodded.

"I wanted to kill him. Because even though I couldn't have you, you were supposed to be mine."

He'd told her Saturday that he'd wanted her back then, but she couldn't remember any sign of it. He'd never once looked at her with desire.

But Eric had. It was the first moment in her life when she'd felt the power of a guy's attraction. And she'd relished it, not because she cared about Eric but because Eric flirting with her had angered Dalton. She was hurt and angry and had wanted to pick a fight. So she'd flirted back.

And that one moment had set the tone for the rest of their high-school years: him silent and brooding, ignoring her and her pushing back, doing one outrageous stunt after another trying to get a reaction out of him. It was a miracle she'd never been kicked out of school for all the stupid crap she'd pulled. Even the principal must have been terrified of Hollister Cain. She'd done it all to get Dalton's attention. And now, she finally had it.

Now she stepped closer to him and put her hand on his face. "I'm sorry," she said simply.

Dalton had always been so self-contained, so emotionally independent. It was hard to imagine that anything she'd done back then had hurt him, but she could see now that it had. "Let's have a do-over. Let's pretend, just for today, that we get to have exactly what those two stupid high-school kids wanted. An afternoon all to ourselves. Completely alone."

It felt like she'd waited forever for Dalton Cain to kiss her. Like she'd been waiting years. Decades. Maybe she had.

The sheer romanticism of the day hit her hard in the solar plexus. The breeze, the ocean, his words. Him. Everything he said—about how he didn't bring other women here, about how long he'd wanted her—sent her alarm bells ringing. This did not sound like the kind of casual fling she could easily walk away from. Which meant she should be using her Get Out of Jail Free card. Do not pass Go. Do not collect $200.

So why wasn't she?

Everything in her life was suddenly so confusing. This was supposed to be a breezy affair. Then again, she was supposed to hate Dalton.

Of course, now she understood the truth. It wasn't that she hated him. He was the cupcake on the other side of the bakery window—perfect, delicious and forever completely out of reach. She hadn't hated the cupcake. She'd hated the glass.

And now that glass was gone. All those years of longing just rushed in. Her hand nearly trembled when she reached up to touch his face. Nearly? No, it trembled—noticeably. And she couldn't seem to stop it.

She should have tried harder to still her hand and to resist him. Normally, she *would* have tried. But the way he looked at her…oh, God, the way he looked at her stripped away the last of her will.

She'd given him the perfect invitation to just kiss her. But instead of taking it, instead of kissing her until she was thoughtless with passion, instead of taking her right there on the deck, he was just standing there, holding her, looking at her like she was...well, like *she* was the cupcake.

How was it that they'd both waited so long? How had they both wanted this so badly and not acted before now? How had they stood it?

Rising up onto her toes, she pressed her mouth to his. It was not the hard, passionate rush she'd been expecting just a moment ago, but a kiss as gentle and as beautiful as the ocean spray.

It was only a brief, delicate hint of a kiss. And then she stepped away, because she couldn't bear to rush this. She couldn't bear to get it wrong.

There were so many reasons why they couldn't have a real relationship. So many people and things that stood between them. So many words and lies. So many deceptions.

But right here on this boat. Right now in this moment... they could have this. It could never be forever, but it could be enough.

So she extracted herself from his arms and—without saying another word—walked down the ladder to the lower deck. Just as she'd suspected, the tiny galley and living area led to a berth at the bow of the boat.

Despite the room's luxury, it was tiny, with space for little other than the bed. She was pulling her shirt over her head when she heard him close the door behind him.

She let her shirt drop to the floor, and still, she didn't stop to see if he was there watching her undress. Her body was so finely tuned to his that she knew he was there without needing to see him. Maybe she didn't turn around because she didn't need to. Maybe it was because she was too nervous.

Or it could be that she didn't want to be swept away. She didn't want wild, raging, out-of-control passion. She wanted slow and steady. She wanted heat without getting burned. She wanted his body without losing her soul.

She dropped her hands to the waistband of her shorts, but her fingers felt clumsy, or maybe the button was just caught. Or maybe her hands were shaking too much. Because she was undressing in front of Dalton Cain.

She sucked in a long, deep breath, trying to still the tremor in her hands, trying to sublimate her jitters beneath the thrum of her desire. The button finally slipped free, and she shimmied out of her shorts.

That's when she felt him behind her—just the barest of touches. He ran something—a fingertip, maybe?—down the length of her back, from the nape of her neck all the way down to the elastic of her panties. He detoured briefly to trace the outline of the tattoo on her shoulder. A delicate sprig of forget-me-nots. His finger was warm and a little rough—like he did more with his hands than just pushing papers. Then he slipped his finger under the waistband of her panties, running his knuckle back and forth across the sensitive skin of her lower back. The gesture started small and slow, just an inch or so of movement. But with each pass, the arc grew bigger, sweeping to trail across more and more of her back.

Then she felt his lips on the back of her neck. The moist pressure of his mouth against the delicate skin just below her ear. The tender nip of his teeth.

She shivered. There were no nerves this time—just pleasure.

And then his hand slipped around to the front of her. Just under the waistband of her panties, his fingertips traced the shape of her hip bone, pressing gently into the sensitive flesh of her lower abdomen. The shiver pulsing through her body made her ache. She could feel the heat swirling through her, the blood pooling in the folds of her femininity. Instinctively, she arched her back. Her buttocks bumped against him.

He was right behind her—so close she could feel his erection against her. But, she realized somewhat stupidly, of course he was that close. His mouth was on her neck. His hands were on her hips. It felt as though he was everywhere. As though he was exactly where he was meant to be.

She was letting him in now, and it felt as though she had no choice in the matter, as though this moment had been destined. Then his hand slipped lower, between her legs, to the nub of her desire. Again, she arched against him, pressing herself to him. His mouth was at her ear, murmuring to her—nothing of momentous importance, the sweetest of nothings. But the tone of his voice—all rough and gravel—felt almost as good as his fingers stroking her.

Then his hand slipped lower, one finger thrusting into her. A full body shudder coursed through her as she moaned aloud. And suddenly, the slow pace she thought she wanted wasn't enough at all. She was on fire—desperate as she rocked against him.

"I need you," she gasped out. "Now."

"I know," he murmured in her ear. "Soon."

She tried to turn to face him. But he held her firmly where she was, stroking her nub, pushing her closer and closer to the edge. She resisted for only an instant before she gave in. She raised her foot up to the edge of the bed, giving Dalton better access as he stroked and thrust, his movements both tender and fierce. She relished the feeling of him right behind her, the strength of him at her back, the agility of his hands as he slowly pushed her over the edge into ecstasy.

Then, a moment later, as she was still trembling, he pressed his hand against her back, bending her over at the waist, and then entered her from behind. So close on the heels of her last orgasm, sensation rocketed through her. She bucked back against him, meeting him thrust for thrust, arching and squirming as she felt herself clenching around him. She reached her own hand back through the folds of her flesh to find the same spot he'd stroked so attentively just a moment before. She climaxed a second time just as she felt him clench her hips and call out her name.

Eleven

Dalton knew they had to return to civilization sometime. If he'd had his druthers, that time would be in about sixteen years—sixteen days, at least. But he didn't think he could talk Laney into an impromptu vacation.

She'd dozed off after they'd made love a second time, and though he'd hated to do it, he'd left her side, dressed and gone up to the captain's deck to take them back to the marina. She woke when they were still about thirty minutes away and followed him up onto the deck. She said nothing but came to stand behind him, wrapping her arms around his waist and resting her cheek against his back as she stared out the window at the slowly setting sun.

Unlike most people, she seemed at peace with the silence of the ocean. Or maybe she didn't think they had anything else to say. Or maybe it was the opposite. Maybe she thought they had too much to say, which, when he thought about it, seemed all too true.

She didn't speak until after he'd eased the boat into the slip, then jumped onto the deck to tie up the boat.

As he was climbing back onto the yacht, she sent a longing glance out at the ocean and sighed. "I almost don't want to go ashore."

"We don't have to."

"Right. We'll live at sea from now on."

"I didn't mean forever," he said. "Tempting though that may be."

"Right. Like you're going to just walk away from your job."

"I said it was tempting. Not irresistible. But actually what I meant was that we don't have to go ashore tonight. There's no reason we can't stay here for the night. As long as you're willing to get up early in the morning to drive back into Houston, we don't have to leave until morning."

He expected her to say no, to argue about the logistics of it, but instead, she just cocked her head to the side and asked, "You think we could get someone to deliver a pizza out to your boat?"

"Oh, I think we can do considerably better than that." He tugged on her hand and led her back down below deck to the galley. "I think I saw some eggs in the fridge."

She dug her heels in on the last step of the ladder. "Eggs? As in cooking? I've got to warn you, I can't cook. Literally can't boil an egg."

"Anyone can boil an egg."

"Not me." She waved her hand in a "what can I say?" gesture. "Why do you think I wanted to order a pizza?"

He gave her hand another tug, and she stumbled down the last step of the ladder. "Here, you sit and watch. I think I can manage an egg or two."

Instead of sitting on the bench seat, Laney sat on the table, propping her feet on the seat. Because the living space and galley of the ship were so confined, he was only a step or two away in the galley. He surveyed the contents of the fridge, pulling out the box of eggs he'd seen earlier, along with a shallot, some fresh spinach, bacon, salsa and cheese. Since there was limited counter space, he set most of the ingredients on the table beside Laney and then put the bacon on to fry.

Laney watched him with an expression of bemused confusion. When he pulled out the chef's knife and started dicing the shallot, she dropped her head into her hands and shook her head. "You know, I'm actually kind of embarrassed," she choked out past what was either nervous giggling or sobs of frustration.

"Why?" he asked.

"Because I can't cook at all and you—" she gestured to the ingredients out on the counter "—can do all this."

"I'm just making a frittata. It's not that impressive."

"It's impressive enough. I don't even know what a frittata is."

"It's a lazy man's omelet. Doesn't require flipping, which is always the hard part."

"Well, I'm still embarrassed. I should be able to do something in the kitchen besides dialing Papa Murphy's."

"You shouldn't be. No one could blame you for not cooking on top of everything you do in a day."

She scoffed dismissively. "I don't—"

"I've seen everything you do in a day. You teach school and run the afterschool program. And you take care of your grandmother. I bet you see her every evening, don't you?" He didn't give her a chance to answer. She would just deny it, but he'd know she was lying, because he knew she'd been over at Restful Hills once a day in the time since he'd been back in her life.

"It's not a burden," Laney said.

He stepped back over to the two-burner cooktop to check on the bacon. "You don't have to pretend with me."

"It really isn't." Her voice was soft, thoughtful—not the normal hollow protestation you might expect from a caregiver.

He shot her a look.

She made a choking sound, somewhere between a giggle

and gag. "I guess that sounds crazy, doesn't it? Me saying it's not a burden. It's just that—"

"Don't forget, I've seen Matilda at her worst. You can't pretend that's easy."

"No, it's not! It's just…things have never been easy between us. I mean, do you remember what it was like when I was teenager?"

He did remember. Laney and her grandmother had had rousing, full-pitch arguments that nearly shook the rafters—seemingly about everything from the way Laney dressed and wore her hair to the guys she dated. He'd always been surprised that no one else in his household seemed to notice or care how badly they got along, but he'd certainly paid attention. The few times he'd tried to make things better, by intervening on her behalf, he'd only made things much worse.

"We fought. All the time. And we just…don't anymore. Or only very rarely. Maybe she isn't the grandmother I knew, but that's not such a bad thing. Some days I go to visit and she doesn't know me at all. She's as polite to me as she would be to a stranger. Other days, she thinks I'm Elaine, and she treats me like the sister she lost. It sounds so tragic when I say it aloud but isn't really. I get the chance to know her as someone else entirely. As someone she loved and cherished. I get to see this side of her I never imagined was there."

He stopped chopping the shallots to turn and look at Laney. Her expression was wistful and sad but not beaten. Leave it to Laney to find an upside to this horrible disease.

She glanced up then and seemed to realize he was watching her, because she gave a nervous little laugh and tucked her hair behind her ear. "Don't get me wrong. I wouldn't wish this on anyone. It's a horrible, tragic disease, but…" Laney made a quick furtive motion, and he thought she brushed a tear away. "I don't know. She's lost so many people she loved. Her sister, her husband, her son. On the days she remembers the best, those are the hard days. The days she's most bitter.

She has fewer and fewer days where she remembers. Maybe it's easier for her this way. That's what I tell myself anyway."

Maybe he should have left it alone. But despite Laney's reassurances, he couldn't help the anger that surged up inside him on her behalf. "She may have lost a lot of the people she loved, but she still has you. And what you do for her—" he shook his head "—on the days she remembers and knows how much you give up for her, those should be her best days."

Laney actually laughed at that. "Well, sure. In a perfect world. But it's not like I was ever her favorite person. She and I didn't get along from the day I showed up to live with her. I don't know if it was because she disliked my mother so much, if she was angry at being stuck with me after my dad died or maybe she even—" she blew out a shaky breath "—maybe she even resented me for being the one who survived."

There was something so sad in her tone, something so defeated in the tilt of her shoulders. He felt like his heart might break just looking at her. And it was so unlike her. Laney was bubbly life, endless energy, boundless joy. Talking about her grandmother, she looked broken.

And he couldn't really blame her. After all, she'd been eleven when she'd first come to live with her grandmother. She'd just lost her father. As far as he knew, her mother had never been in the picture. And the one family member she still had had frozen her out.

He was struck by a powerful urge to go to her, to wrap her in his arms and just hold her—the kind of spontaneous gesture of affection he was no good at. So instead, he flipped the bacon over one more time and then started moving it out of the pan to the plate.

Laney gave a little shrug. "I know I didn't make things any better. I was a difficult kid."

He spun around, gesturing with the spatula. "Hey, you were a great kid." He might not be much at the spontaneous physical gestures, but he wasn't about to let her take this on herself.

She chuckled. "I was a horrible kid."

"I'm serious. You can't blame yourself. You were just a kid, and you'd lost everything. You may not have been perfect, but she was the adult. Even though she'd just lost her son, she should have been more understanding. Whatever problems there were between you, you weren't to blame."

"Thank you." Her words were simple, but her eyes were glowing warmly and her tone was thick with meaning.

Suddenly there was a lump in his throat, and he turned back to cooking before swallowing it. He scraped the chopped shallot into the bacon grease before saying, "You're welcome."

As he pushed the shallots around the pan, he heard her hop down off the table. A moment later, he felt her arms snake around him, and she once against rested her cheek against his back.

That tight feeling in his chest loosened. He might not be good at the spontaneous gestures of affection, but she was great at them.

He flicked off the heat beneath the shallots and turned to wrap her in his arms. She tilted her head up, and he automatically dropped his mouth to hers. Once again, he was amazed by how perfect she tasted, how ideally she fit in his arms, like she was made just for him. He backed her up a step or two until he was able to lift her so she once again sat on the table. Her legs immediately went around his waist, and she used them to tug him even closer. He felt desire stirring inside him. He'd spent the whole afternoon making love to her. How could he want her again so soon? Of course, the answer was obvious.

He could want her again so soon because he'd always wanted her. He would always want her. It was as simple and as complicated as that. She was his.

Laney arched her arms over her head, stretching out tired muscles before pulling her shirt back on. Before she could get the hem all the way down, Dalton's hand sneaked under and cupped her breast again. She gave him a playful swat. "Hands to yourself until you've fed me at least."

As if to make her point, her stomach growled. Dalton leaned down and kissed her belly. "Your wish is my command."

She laughed at his joke, but somewhere, deep inside, his words stirred up her doubts. All playfulness aside, her wishes were going to get her into serious trouble. The last time she'd felt like this about a guy, the last time she'd been in a make-love-three-times-a-day kinda relationship, she'd been in college and she'd ended up with her heart so broken she'd nearly flunked out. It scared her to think she might be going down that road again.

Here, now, out on the boat, making love over and over... this was the stuff of fantasies, but she knew she was living on borrowed time. Too many things—too many lies—stood between them. This just couldn't last. Pretending that it could, even for a night, was dangerous—for her heart, anyway.

"Hey, why do you look so serious?" he asked, pulling his own shirt back on.

What was she supposed to say to that? I'm afraid you're too perfect? I'm afraid of falling in love with you? Yeah... way to be cool.

So she forced a grin. "The only thing I'm serious about is eating and you owe me a fri...omelet thingy."

"A frittata."

"Right. Now get cooking."

By the time they were sitting at the table with the frittatas in front of them, she'd finally worked up the nerve to ask the question that was niggling at the back of her mind. "Tell me about Portia."

"What about her?"

"Did you love her?"

Love? What did he know of love at twenty-two? Or now for that matter? "I believed we were well matched."

"So that's a no."

"Why does it matter?"

"I don't know if it does. But you were married to her for

eight years. That's…longer than some presidents serve. That's longer than anything I've done in my life. Yet when you talk about her, I hear nothing in your voice. No passion. No hatred. No love. No regret. Just nothing."

"What do you want to hear? Do you want me to be obsessing about her? Plotting her murder?"

"I don't know. Something. Something that shows me you cared for her even a little bit. You had to have had some reason for marrying her. Some reason to stay married that long. Some reason for leaving her. Something."

He blew out a frustrated breath and ran a hand through his hair. "Look, I married her because I was supposed to. She had been born, bred and educated to make the perfect wife for a man like me. She's beautiful. She had the right connections. She knew all the same people I knew. It just made sense."

"Did she make you happy?"

"I wasn't raised to believe happiness was important. Or even real. You live up to your responsibilities. You find satisfaction in your work. You devote your life to the company and do everything in your power to protect those under you. Notions like happiness and love are myths spun to placate the middle and lower classes."

She sank back against the chair. "And that's what you believe."

"That's what I was raised to believe. I grew up thinking love was just a convenient word people use to describe physical desire. Emotions are weakness. You wouldn't choose a life partner based on love any more than you'd purchase a company because their logo was aesthetically pleasing."

She shook her head, trying to sort through all the emotional clutter his words stirred up. "If all that's true, then why did you leave her?"

"I didn't. She left me. Which was a blessing in disguise because she never made me happy. But I'd married her. I was just trying to make it work."

"Why did she leave you?"

"I always thought it was enough that we were a good match. Turns out it wasn't enough for her. She wanted more. She wanted kids. We couldn't have them together. She wanted more from me than I was able to give."

Laney was quiet for a long moment, looking down at her frittata, poking it listlessly with her fork. "I see."

He hadn't been able to love the woman he'd been married to for eight years. If the stunningly beautiful, coolly sophisticated, insanely perfect Portia hadn't been able to win his heart, then she certainly never would.

Before she could contemplate that grim thought anymore, he reached across the table and tipped her chin up so that she met his gaze. "I wished I could have given her what she needed emotionally. I tried to, but it just wasn't there. It never was. If I'd known she wanted love, I never would have married her. I knew going into this with you that you'd never be satisfied with half measures. I hurt Portia. I don't want to hurt you."

Her heart swelled even more, past the point of comfort, to the point where she felt like she was being choked. She couldn't escape from the intensity of his gaze—not when he was this close and the quarters were so tight.

"Stop," she said.

"Stop what?" he asked.

"Just stop, okay?" She pushed her plate away. "Stop acting like this is more than it is. Stop acting like you care about me."

"Why? I do care about you, Laney. Why are you having such a hard time dealing with that?"

Twelve

He reached for her hand, and she jerked it away, so he placed his palm flat down on the table.

She shoved her chair back with her legs and stood. "No. No, you don't really care about me. You've just come back into my life. It's only been, what? Five days? You don't care about me. You barely know me."

He smiled, looking a little bemused. "You don't get to tell me how I feel."

"You barely know me," she repeated, enunciating the words clearly, willing him to read between the lines, willing him to turn tail and run, which was precisely what he should do.

But of course, he didn't. Dalton wasn't the kind of man to be easily scared off. Besides, he didn't know about the oceans of lies between them. He didn't know that Gran had stolen money from his parents. He didn't know that Laney had been working to cover it up.

And even if he did know about all that, they still couldn't

be together. Because she knew the truth, even if he wasn't ready to face it yet. They didn't belong together.

"Look, Dalton, you've said it yourself. Every decision you've made since you were seven has been focused on how to make you a better CEO for Cain Enterprises, which made you the least rebellious teenager in the history of the world."

"What does that have to do with anything?"

"It has everything to do with us. You're the one who admitted that you cut me out of your life because I could never be part of your five-year plan."

"That's not what I said."

"Those weren't the words you used, but that's what it boiled down to. And that's why how you're acting now makes perfect sense. You didn't pursue me when you were a teenager, because it wasn't part of your plan to be the perfect CEO. But as soon as your father threatened to cut you off, you came looking for me. I'm your big teenage rebellion. You're just going through it sixteen years too late."

"That's not true."

"It is. And I don't even mind. You deserve to cut loose a little. If anyone deserves to play hooky on a Monday afternoon, it's you. And trust me, I'm thrilled I'm the girl you picked to play hooky with. But don't pretend it's anything more. Don't lie to me."

"I'm not lying to you."

"Then you're lying to yourself."

"You're wrong."

Laughter burst out of her, and she was shocked by how maniacal it sounded. "I wish I was. You don't think I wish the handsome, rich man of my dreams really cared about me? 'Cause I do."

"Laney…" He reached for her, but she skittered out of his grasp.

"I absolutely wish that just for once my life could be as simple as that. But this is *my* life we're talking about. And things like love and relationships and people staying around when they say they're going to…that kind of thing just doesn't work out for me. So you'll just have to excuse me if instead of getting swept up into the fantasy of sailing off into the sunset with you—literally sailing off into the sunset!—I concentrate on the facts as I know them."

He looked like he was clenching his jaw. When he spoke, his tone was sharp and terse. "And what are the facts as you know them?"

"You may desire me, but you don't really care about me—"

"Don't tell me how I feel."

"Because if you did, you wouldn't have waited to come find me. My path and yours crossed for one reason. Because your father issued this stupid edict that you find the missing heiress. If your father hadn't ordered you to find her… If my grandmother didn't have Alzheimer's and could have spoken to you herself… If I'd never moved back to Houston… If any of that had been the case, we would have gone the rest of our lives without ever seeing each other again."

"You don't know that."

"I know that if you hadn't practically stumbled over me, I wouldn't be out on your boat now. I know that if you were half as crazy about me as—" she broke off, because she very nearly said, "as I am about you." Instead she finished the sentence with "—as you claim to be, then you would have come and found me before now."

"Is that what you believe? That I should have come to find you the second the ink was dry on my divorce papers? It hasn't even been a year yet. In fact, it's been less than nine months."

The hard note in his voice sent a thread of doubt through her, but she quickly pushed it aside. "That's long enough."

"Okay, you tell me. How long should I have waited. Six months? Three months? Or maybe even that's too long. Maybe I should have gone straight from the lawyer's office to your duplex after I signed the papers. Maybe I should have called you right after she kicked me out of the house. But let's see, my marriage had just ended. I had nowhere to live. Hollister had just had the first of his heart attacks less than three months before that. I was working eighteen-hour days. Is that when I should have called you?"

She gritted her teeth as he spoke. She couldn't make herself stop listening to his words, but she desperately wished she didn't have to hear them. He sounded so logical.

He was not cold or dispassionate and not uncaring. She could have hated him for that. But instead, his arguments just made sense.

Damn.

"What, Laney? No witty comeback? Nothing to put me in my place?"

"I'm right," she said, clenching her arms tightly across her middle. "I know I'm right."

He stopped pacing to stand in front her. She refused to look at him, because she didn't think she could bear to see the pleading in his eyes, couldn't bear to want to trust him, not when she knew what a mistake it would be to do so.

He carefully disentangled her arms so that he could clasp her hands. "Did it ever occur to you that I didn't come and find you before now because I needed the excuse? I'm not an idiot. I knew that by the end of high school you hated me. Hell, when I walked up outside the school last Thursday, you looked ready to choke me. If I hadn't had a legitimate reason to talk to you, how long do you think you would have stayed around? If I'd asked you out on a date, what would you have said?"

"Well, I guess we'll never know, will we?" Her words sounded weak and trembly. She wanted to be fierce. She wanted to channel all the rebellious fire that had burned through her as a teenager. She wanted to curse and throw things at him and spit on his shoes.

She meant her words to be a challenge, an insult.

Instead they were her regrets laid bare.

Suddenly she felt far too vulnerable. She wanted so much from him that he could never give her.

She turned back around to him, facing him fully, looking

him in the eye for the first time in this discussion. "I can't stay here."

Again, he reached for her, and again, she dodged out of his grasp. He sighed, and it sounded as resigned as she felt. "Okay, I'll drive you back."

Great, just what she needed: an hour in the car with him.

Next time she decided to get her heart broken, she was going to do it closer to home. Stupid friggin' yacht.

Before she could think it through, she marched up the steps to the deck and hopped off the boat onto the dock. Funny all the nerves and insecurity she had to overcome to even get on the damn boat. Was it a sign she'd grown that she was able to get off it so easily?

"Wait, Laney," he called from behind her. "I can't leave yet. Give me five minutes, ten max."

"No," she said. "Forget it. I'm not riding back to Houston with you anyway."

"You can't walk."

"I'll go to the office. Have them call me a cab."

"A cab?" he repeated, infusing the word with such repulsion she might as well have said she'd lick the ground all the way back to her duplex. "You can't take a cab back to Houston. For starters, it would cost a fortune."

"So?" He was right, of course. She so didn't have the money for a hundred-dollar cab ride.

"Let me drive you." He must have seen the refusal in her eyes, because he held up his hand in resignation. "Or, you take the car yourself."

"I'm not taking your car. You'd be stuck there."

"I'll call Sydney," he said. "She can have a company driver come pick me up within the hour."

Still she hesitated. She didn't like being dependent on anyone, especially Dalton because she was already so deeply in his debt.

"Think of it as blackmail." He pulled his keys out of his

pocket and tossed them to her. "This way I'll have to see you again sometime."

"I'll be sure to gas it up before I return it," she said snidely.

Dalton just shook his head, his expression sad. "What, now you're giving me hell for wanting to take care of you?"

"I've been on my own since I was seventeen." The anger in her voice shocked her. But there was sorrow in there too. And pain. Those were the emotions that terrified her. She swallowed hard and didn't speak until she was sure her voice would sound crystal clear and void of emotion. "I do just fine taking care of myself. If you want something to take care of, buy a terrier."

She turned then, ready to stalk off to his car, but then she saw the name sprawled on the prow of the boat and stopped still in her tracks. Despite the turmoil of her emotions, her brain started clicking, making rapid-fire connections.

She looked up at Dalton. He was staring at her, confusion furrowing his brow. Clearly he could tell something had stumped her.

"You said this was your father's boat and you bought it from him?"

"Yes. Why?"

She didn't answer but turned and walked off down the dock. She heard him hop off the boat to see what she'd been looking at. Either he'd figure it out or he wouldn't.

As for her, she did what she always had. She just kept moving. She'd driven a lot of different cars over the years—her own, rentals, cars owned by guys she'd dated. So she was comfortable enough around cars that Dalton's seventy-thousand-dollar luxury sedan didn't give her much trouble. She started it up, adjusted the seat and immediately turned on the radio, flipping through stations until she reached the alt-rock she liked. Then she cranked it up loud. She tore out of the parking lot, pausing only long enough for the security guard to open the gate. The guy looked a little surprised, but he let her through. Either he worried she was stealing Dalton's car or the marina full of two-million-dollar yachts didn't hear a lot of Seether—probably both.

She zipped up Highway 45 toward Houston, driving too fast with the windows rolled down and the music too loud, half hoping she'd get pulled over. But no one stopped her, and soon, she was chilly and her head started to ache. But she kept driving, and she wasn't even tempted to cry until she pulled up in front of her duplex.

Then she just sat there in the car, squeezing her eyes tight to trap the tears inside. 'Cause she so didn't want any of her neighbors to see her coming home late at night, tear-stained and windblown.

She had known this thing with Dalton would never last. She'd known it was just a temporary distraction in her life. So why did it hurt? Why did she feel like her heart was breaking?

God, she hated being reduced to clichés. And suddenly her whole life seemed like a cliché: girl from the wrong side of the tracks and the rich business tycoon. God, it had all the makings of a Doris Day movie. All it lacked was the happy ending.

Too bad she wasn't Doris Day. She wasn't virginal, she wasn't plucky and she couldn't sing, which sucked, 'cause she could really use a rousing rendition of "Que Sera, Sera" right now.

She was standing on the porch of her half of the duplex when she finally lost the battle with her tears. It was the keys that tipped her over the edge. She'd left her purse—and therefore her keys—on Dalton's boat...stupid yacht. And she hadn't even realized it until she'd made it home because she was driving his stupid Lexus.

Sinking down onto the top step of her porch, she considered her options. She had no wallet and no cash, so she couldn't just get a hotel for the night. The sofa in Gran's living room pulled out. She'd slept on it enough times that no one at Restful Hills would think twice about her showing up. But what if Matilda was having a bad day? Laney didn't think she had the energy to deal with any more drama. She'd seemed fine that morning when Laney had been there, but who knew if her day had taken a turn for the worse. Laney's certainly had.

She clenched her hand, and Dalton's keys bit into her palm. Opening her fist, she thumbed through them. There was the key to the Lexus, as well as three others. One of them had to be the key to his house...no, not his house. Hadn't he said he lived in a condo? It would be somewhere downtown—probably one of the new buildings that had gone up in the past few years, but she had no way of knowing which one. Even if she wanted to stay at his place and risk having him come home in the middle of the night, she couldn't stay there because she didn't even know where he lived. She'd slept with him, and she didn't even have his address. How pathetic was she?

She'd dropped her head in her hands, and the tears had started to fall in earnest when suddenly she felt a hand on her shoulder. She jerked to her feet and whirled around only to find Brandon standing there. Though their front doors were on different sides of the cottage, they shared a wraparound porch.

Brandon took one look at her, pulled her into his arms and just held her, letting her cry. A few minutes later, she'd told him the whole thing and nearly made herself sick crying so much, but she felt marginally better. Brandon, on the other hand, was looking at her like she was crazy.

"I'm not making any sense, am I?" she asked.

"Perfect sense," he reassured her. "Handsome, rich guy declares his love. Bleck. Who would want that?"

"No, seriously, you think I'm crazy, don't you?"

Brandon tilted his head to the side and studied her for a minute. "No. I don't. You're a pretty good judge of character. If you think he's an ass, then he's probably an ass."

She shook her head. "It's not that he's an ass. I just don't think he's going to stick around."

"Honey, if a guy says he cares about you, seduces you and then doesn't stick around, he's an ass."

She opened her mouth to protest again—because that wasn't really what had happened—but she closed it without saying anything. She *couldn't* say anything. She couldn't defend Dalton without admitting the truth. He hadn't dumped her. She'd dumped him. It had been a defensive, preventive dumping, but still…

Was it unfair of her to run before he could walk away from her? No. She was only protecting herself.

He would leave her—eventually.

A few years from now, Dalton would marry again. He was too practical not to. It would be someone like Portia—maybe a little younger but someone like her. Beautiful. Rich. Connected. Someone who knew how to be the perfect wife of a CEO, someone with the right kind of social ambitions, someone who didn't teach first grade and didn't run afterschool drama programs. And that someone would never be her.

Maybe she was being unfair to Dalton. Maybe she was judging the man he was now based on the actions of the boy he'd been when he had befriended and then dumped her. Maybe that was unfair.

But he'd dumped her because he knew—even at the age of sixteen—that she didn't have what it took to be the girlfriend of a future CEO. She still didn't have what it took.

Finally Brandon rubbed her arm and helped her to her feet. "Come on, I'll get you my spare key." As he let her into his half of the duplex, he asked, "So what are you going to do?"

She shrugged. "About what?"

"This is Dalton Cain we're talking about here. He's not just going to let you walk away. If he wants you, he's going to fight for you. Are you strong enough to keep telling him no?"

"Yeah. I am. But I won't have to tell him no for long. As soon as he's back in his father's good graces, he'll come to his senses."

"That's assuming he finds the missing heiress and gets back into his father's good graces. If what you told me just now is true, that's a pretty big assumption. You have no idea who this girl is. You don't even know when she was born."

"That's true, but I think I know who the girl's mother is."

"You do?"

"Yeah."

Laney thought back to the moment she was leaving Dalton on the boat. It was the first time she noticed the yacht's name: Victoria III.

That boat had been Hollister Cain's boat. And since Dalton had bought the boat from his father right after his divorce—when Dalton had been working eighteen-hour days—she was guessing Dalton hadn't bothered to rename it.

Boats were always named after women. So the Caroline or the Caro would have been logical choices, after his wife. But Hollister hadn't named his boat that. Instead, he'd gone with Victoria III. Whoever Victoria was, she must have meant a lot to Hollister. He'd named not one but three boats after her. And whoever she was, Laney was guessing that she sometimes went by the name Vee.

Of course, Laney knew that even if she did help Dalton find the heiress, things would never be truly right between them because she still wouldn't be able to tell him about the money that Gran had stolen. As long as Gran was alive, she could never be completely honest about that. Not that it really mattered when she came clean about the money. There was no point in her future when she could tell him about the money and expect his forgiveness. She'd been silent too long on that front.

No, at some point, after Gran had passed, she'd find a way to tell him. She'd face the consequences. She only hoped that helping him find the heiress now would soften the blow when it came. She only hoped that the hatred he would surely feel for her then wouldn't hurt her as much as his affection did now.

Thirteen

Tuesday morning, after arranging to have Laney's purse sent by courier over to her duplex—because he assumed he was the last person she'd want to see—he took a cab to his parents' house.

He knew if he went after her now, she'd just bolt. So he would wait and let her cool down a bit. He had all the time in the world. She'd realize soon enough that he wasn't going anywhere. Hollister Cain had always had a penchant for expensive cars. No one would notice if Dalton borrowed one until Laney returned his. But the car was secondary. Dalton pocketed a set of keys from the hooks in the pantry and then made his way to his father's ad hoc hospital room at the front of the house.

He entered and was greeted by the usual chorus of beeps and drips and the sight of his father sitting up in bed. Though Hollister's eyes were closed, he appeared healthier than he had in some time, despite the oxygen tube that crisscrossed under his nose and the IV strapped to his arm.

Dalton hesitated by the door. He had to talk to Hollister, but his father needed his rest more, and perhaps his mother would have the information he was looking for.

Just as Dalton was turning to leave, Hollister spoke. "Apparently you misunderstood my orders. You should be out looking for the heiress, not lounging in my doorway like a puppy dog."

Dalton stifled the anger that spiked through him. Hollister understood exactly one motivational technique: domination. He used it to control his employees, his wife and his children.

Sometimes Dalton was amazed that his father's business had been as successful as it was, given how ineffective his leadership was.

"Puppies don't lounge," Dalton said, walking in the room. "Old, lazy hound dogs lounge. Puppies bound about and create a mess."

Hollister's eyes fluttered open. "Are you calling me a hound dog?"

"Circumstances being what they are, yes. I think it's appropriate, don't you? Since your hound dogging is what brought us to this."

Hollister chuckled, without a trace of shame. "Touché," he got out before the laughter gave way to coughing. He fumbled at the bedside table for a tissue.

When Hollister stopped coughing, Dalton said, "I need you to tell me about Victoria."

Hollister crumpled the tissue and threw it, not even noticing that he missed the trash can. That was Hollister all over: always content to let others clean up his messes. "Victoria, huh?"

"Yes. Every boat you've owned since the mid-eighties was named Victoria, including the one I just bought from you. I want to know who Victoria is."

Hollister coughed again, but this time it sounded forced, as if he was stalling. He tossed another tissue to the ground.

"Son, you sure picked a strange time to walk down memory lane."

Son...that's how Dalton knew he was onto something. His father never pulled out the good ol' boy colloquialisms unless his back was to the wall.

Dalton sat down in the chair beside the bed, putting him at his father's eye level. This might take some time. "It's not a walk down memory lane. If Victoria is some woman you screwed over, she could be the woman who wrote that letter. She could be the mother of the missing heiress."

Hollister waved his hand dismissively; the gesture was feeble and his hand trembled. Dalton couldn't tell if it was part of the act or if his once-powerful father was really so weak.

"Victoria isn't a woman. Victoria is a town. It's the place where Abel Schwartz and I stayed back in 1982. I thought you knew all about Victoria."

"I do."

Of course he did. The month-long fishing trip that Hollister Cain and Abel Schwartz took back in 1982 was practically a legend within Cain Enterprises. The company had gotten its start back in the forties in the oil fields of east Texas. By the early eighties, Cain Oil & Gas was struggling to compete with the bigger international oil-exploration companies like ARCO and Exxon. The empire Hollister Cain had inherited from his father was starting to flounder, despite the cash he'd infused into the company when he'd married Caroline Dalton.

Then Hollister took a small team of scientists and mathematicians on a fishing trip down on the coast. When they came back, a month later, the team had devised the complex algorithms for graphical-imaging software to aid in oil exploration. A year later, the software had been developed. Cain Oil & Gas got into the exploration-consulting business and became Cain Enterprises. The product shifted the entire focus of the company and put them back on the map. From there, Cain Enterprises branched out into banking and finance as well as land development, while still keeping its thumb in the oil-exploration pie.

Without that software, without that fishing trip, Cain Oil & Gas would have been gobbled up by one of the bigger oil companies. Hollister probably would have stayed on as a VP, but he never would have put his mark on the business world.

"That trip to Victoria made you the businessman you are. In fact, that trip made Cain Enterprises what it is today. Without it, you'd be nothing. So no one ever questioned why you'd name your boats Victoria. I never did."

Hollister nodded slowly, his eyes narrowed to shrewd slits.

"Laney questioned it because she didn't know the story about the trip to Victoria."

"Laney?"

"Laney Fortino. I've been working with her to help figure out who might have sent that letter."

"She some kind of private eye? 'Cause I told you, you can't hire help."

"She's not a P.I. She's a teacher. You know Laney. She's Matilda Fortino's granddaughter." Hollister continued to stare blankly at him, so Dalton added, "She grew up in the carriage house."

Hollister chuffed, which Dalton interpreted as acknowledgment.

"Laney didn't know about the trip to Victoria. She assumed it had to be a woman's name." He left out the part about Matilda and the mysterious person she called Vee. "I knew what Victoria really meant. Or I thought I did."

He was extrapolating, of course, because he hadn't talked to Laney since she'd climbed off his boat. But he'd seen the look on her face when she'd stared at the name scrawled on the prow. After she'd left, he'd hopped off the boat himself and stared at the spot she'd been looking at. It hadn't been hard to imagine her thought process—his father's boat, the name Victoria, which someone might shorten to Vee.

"At first I dismissed it," he told his father, "but then I got to thinking. For the first time, I wondered why you'd go on a fishing trip in Victoria. Victoria is near the coast, but it's not on the coast. In fact, the closest water is Port Lavaca, and that's thirty miles away. I called Abel Schwartz and talked to him first thing this morning."

Abel had retired from Cain over ten years earlier, but Dalton had known him since childhood. Despite his background in science and geology, Schwartz was no absentminded science geek. He'd been as ambitious and ruthless as his father. He was the only member of that team who went on the trip who had stayed at Cain Enterprises for very long.

Hollister's hands clenched his bedcovers, but he gave no other sign he was distressed. "That old fool probably doesn't even remember that trip. He's older than I am and twice as stupid."

"Oh, he remembers the trip. He just doesn't remember it the way you always told it. He claims he didn't stay in Victoria at all. He claims he and the rest of the team stayed in Port Aransas, which is eighty miles from Victoria."

Hollister huffed indignantly. "Abel is a buffoon. He's ninety if he's a day. You think he remembers anything from that trip besides drinking all my scotch?"

"I think it's odd that you'd bring a bunch of scotch on what you later claimed was supposed to be a working trip. More to the point, I think it's even odder that Abel doesn't remember you being there more than a few days."

"He's lying."

"He said you brought the team down, set them up for fishing and then left for three weeks. When you came back, you had a beta version of the exploration software already complete and stored on magnetic tape."

Hollister didn't even flinch. Only the faint beeping of his heart monitor gave him away as the rate of the beeps picked up.

Dalton leaned forward. "Did you steal those algorithms?"

Hollister said nothing.

"Did you steal the ideas on which you built the Cain empire? Dad, I need to know."

Words seemed to catch in Dalton's throat as he said them. How long had it been since he'd called his father that? Years... decades maybe.

Hollister was a ruthless businessman and a disinterested father: an all-around horrible person. But he was still Dalton's father. Dalton needed to know just how bad things were.

Finally Hollister met Dalton's gaze. "What if I did?" he wheezed. "That old man in Victoria, he didn't know what he had on his hands. He was using that software to dig water wells." He gave a grunt of disgust. "Water. When he could be finding oil."

"And that's how you justified stealing?"

"What does it matter? I had employees depending on me. I had a company to save. I did what I needed to do to get the job done. That old man refused to sell me the software. What was I supposed to do?"

Hollister's words shot Dalton straight through the heart. Hadn't he said nearly the same thing to Laney? Hadn't he justified his actions the same way?

At the time, putting the needs of the company—the needs of his many employees—before everything else seemed like the right decision. True, his father's sins were far greater and had benefited far fewer people, but Dalton couldn't deny they were on the same slippery path.

"Did you steal the software?" he asked his father a third time.

"Doesn't really matter, does it?" his father wheezed.

"It matters to me." Dalton pushed himself to his feet and strode to a pair of high arching windows overlooking the palatial front lawn. "After everything I've done for Cain Enterprises..." He knew his father didn't give a damn about his sacrifices. He was just thinking aloud now. "To find out now that it's all built on a lie? How can I lead a company that I no longer believe in?"

Hollister made another gasping sound, and Dalton whirled around. Yeah, it didn't take a genius to figure out that Hollister's days were numbered, but Dalton hoped to hell that today wasn't the day.

However, Hollister wasn't choking or gasping for breath. He seemed to be laughing.

"Nice," Dalton muttered. "I'm in the middle of a moral crisis, and you're laughing at me."

Was it any wonder he wasn't closer to his father?

Dalton's annoyance only gave Hollister's laughter a nastier tone. "If your moral crisis can interrupt my deathbed, then my laughter can interrupt your moral crisis."

"You're not actually on your deathbed," Dalton said wryly, still hoping this was true. "You're too stubborn to die before you've gotten what you want."

Hollister coughed into another tissue. "And what is it you think I want?"

"All of us. Dancing at your whim." He waited for more laughter, but Hollister only lifted one shoulder in a shrug. "What, no laughter? I would have thought that sort of sentimentality would be right up your alley."

"Earlier, I was laughing at you, not your word choice. All those noble ethics of yours." More wheezing laughter from Hollister. "You wouldn't give up Cain Enterprises."

"You don't think I'd walk away from Cain Enterprises?"

"Not over ethics. You don't have the balls to do it. You'll be panting after Cain Enterprises until I pry it out of your hands. But you need to get your ass a'moving, or one of your brothers will find that heiress first."

Dalton just stared at his father. All his life, he'd danced to this man's tune. And what had it gotten him? He had money, certainly, and power, but he had no pride in his work. And now, it turned out, he had no honor either. His father—and Cain Enterprises by association—was responsible for some rather nasty business. This was what he'd fought his whole life for?

"No," he said slowly. "I don't think I will."

With that, he walked out of his father's room. If any more noises came from the room, either gasps or laughter, Dalton blocked it out. He'd made it most of the way down the central hallway when he noticed his mother sitting on the bench in the hall. She stood slowly as he approached.

He nodded in greeting, hoping to keep this short. His mind was buzzing with the information he'd gleaned from Hollister. More than that, energy buzzed through him. The zing of possibility. For the first time in his life, his future held something other than Cain Enterprises.

"Dalton." His mother reached out a hand toward him. "Wait…"

He had little tolerance for his mother's dramatics—especially now. But he stopped and waited for her to speak.

"I heard your conversation with your father."

He hadn't exactly been trying to keep it a secret. "And?"

"And you can't leave Cain Enterprises."

He shoved his hands deep in his pockets. "Hollister doesn't believe I will."

"Hollister isn't thinking clearly. This ridiculous edict of his proves that much." There was a note of anger in his mother's voice that surprised Dalton, something he'd never heard in her voice before, despite all the years of suffering she'd put up with from Hollister. "And he doesn't know any of you boys very well."

"And you know me so much better?"

"I know you have a stubborn streak a mile wide. I know once you decide something you never back down, even when you should." Her fingers tightened on his arm. "Don't make a decision right away. Not about something this important. Don't lose sight of the big picture here. You don't need to be obsessing about the past. You need to be looking for the heiress. And I can help you. I can help you find this girl."

Dalton stopped and turned back toward his mother. "Aah…I see. In other words, Griffin hasn't made any more progress

than I have, and you're starting to get scared—really scared—
that you're about to lose everything or that Cooper will find
her and he'll get the company. I wonder which is worse in
your mind."

His mother stiffened her hands clenching in front of her.
"How like you to make me sound completely heartless. Is it
so hard to believe that I might want you to succeed?"

"It is absolutely that hard to believe. You haven't been in
my corner since I was seven. In all fairness, I haven't been in
yours since then either. But I was just a kid, so I can excuse
my own behavior more easily than yours."

"Fine." She dropped her hands to her sides, but there was
no acquiescence in her voice, only stubborn pride. "Hate me
if you need to, but there's no need to punish yourself. You
still love Cain Enterprises. I know you do. And the company
needs you."

"Cain Enterprises doesn't need me." Saying the words
aloud should have hurt. Somehow, it didn't. "Cain will be
okay. It'll be just fine with Griffin at the helm. Even Cooper
for that matter."

"What about if neither of them comes through? What if
your father dies and leaves everything to the state to be auc-
tioned off? You know Sheppard Capital will be first in line to
snap up those stocks, and Grant Sheppard will be more than
happy to run this company into the ground."

"And I don't care." He spoke slowly, biting out each word.
"I'm disgusted with how Hollister did business. I'm done."

"Why?" she demanded. "Because you think you've fallen
in love? You think love is going to make you a better man?"

"I didn't say I loved her." Of course, he did love her, but
he certainly didn't want to hand that kind of ammunition to
his mother.

She just scoffed. "You didn't have to say it. There's only
one thing that would make you all dewy-eyed with morality."

"I wasn't going to trot out all the old clichés, but yes, I do want to be a better man. Certainly a better man than Hollister is."

His mother gave an elegant huff of disapproval. "Do you think she's so pure and honest? Your father might not remember her, but I do. That little slut was sniffing around you from the day she moved here."

"Don't try to sully my opinion of her with your lies."

He fully expected some defensive backpedalling, but instead his mother's gaze went cold. "I don't have to lie to make her look bad. Her grandmother has done enough on that count."

"Her grandmother? You mean the woman who ran your household seamlessly for thirty years? That woman?"

"I mean the woman who's stolen hundreds of thousands of dollars from this family."

For a long moment, Dalton just stared blankly at his mother, then he turned around and kept walking down the hall, chuckling under his breath.

"You don't believe me?" his mother demanded.

"Of course I don't believe you. Matilda Fortino was practically a saint. She would never steal, let alone from you."

"I'm not lying. I can prove it." His mother's eyes were lit with fervor.

In thirty-two years, he'd never seen his mother this desperate. "Okay, I'll bite. Why do you think our loyal housekeeper—a woman you trusted for thirty years, a woman who practically raised your children for you—is a thief?"

"Over the last several years she worked here, over half a million dollars went missing from the household accounts. Only three people had access to that money—Matilda, your father and I."

"Maybe Hollister—"

"When did Hollister ever care what went on under this roof?"

He could barely wrap his mind around the accusations his mother was making. The idea that stern and serious Matilda had embezzled money from the family was…bizarre to say the least.

Matilda had always had an almost puritanical moral code. He'd once seen her leave insurance information after dinging a car in a store parking lot. She was the kind of woman who counted her change and gave back the extra dime. She wasn't the kind of woman who stole from her employers.

On the other hand, his mother was the kind of woman who would stretch the truth to manipulate people. She was even the kind who would lie outright…but not about something anyone could verify. She would never mention numbers and household accounts if she didn't have proof to back it up.

For the moment, he pushed aside the question of whether or not his mother was lying. "Even if you are right, what does that have to do with anything? So what if Matilda stole a half-million dollars from you? So what if she stole a million dollars? That doesn't have anything to do with Laney. Even you can't judge Laney based on something her grandmother did."

Satisfaction flared in his mother's eyes. He almost knew what he was going to say before she said it. "Who do you think takes care of Matilda's finances now that she's in that home?"

Dalton felt the fire that had been driving him all morning flicker. He said nothing. He didn't have to. His mother plowed ahead, making her point.

"For three years now, Laney is the only one who could be managing her money. Laney is the one who moved Matilda into Restful Hills. Without the money Matilda stole from us, Laney wouldn't even be able to afford to have put her there. Can you honestly tell yourself that Laney didn't know the money was stolen?"

No. He couldn't.

Mock pity laced Caro's voice. "She had to know where that money came from. She had to know her grandmother was a thief. And she never even told you, did she?" The pity turned icy cold as she drove her point home. "Do you want to tell me again how innocent your girlfriend is?"

For a long time, Dalton just stood there in shock, his mother's words filtering through his mind. He ignored the grim satisfaction on her face. Ignored her obvious glee at his turmoil. He even ignored the pain stabbing through him.

Laney didn't trust him. She never had. The woman he'd held in his arms just last night, the woman he'd made love to, the woman he'd loved, didn't trust him enough to tell him this herself.

He ruthlessly shoved that painful realization aside. Because no matter what else happened, no matter what the fallout was from that realization, he was absolutely certain of one thing: his father's bedroom door was still open. His mother had dropped this bombshell within hearing range of Hollister.

Despite his failing health, despite the heart attacks, despite the weakening lungs, there was one body part that still worked perfectly. Hollister's ears.

Dalton spun on his heels and stalked back into Hollister's room. He didn't stop until he was leaning over his father's bed, staring the old man right in his eyes. Hollister's gaze was lit with an unholy satisfaction. He loved Dalton's anguish even more than Caro had. He practically cackled with joy. Why wouldn't he? He now had another string he could jerk to manipulate Dalton.

Had Hollister been any healthier, Dalton would have been tempted to jerk the old man up by the collar and give him a fierce shake. As it was, he had to satisfy himself with mere words.

"I know you heard what Caro just said. Do not think for one minute that you can use this information to control me. If you go after Laney or her grandmother, I will—"

"What?" Hollister barked. "I'm damn near dead. There's not a damn thing you can do to me."

"Trust me. I'll find something. I will find out the truth about what you did in Victoria and I'll make it common knowledge. I'll besmirch your memory. I'll find a way to dismantle Cain Enterprises brick by brick until everything you've done in your life has been destroyed. Do you understand me?"

Hollister's smile only widened. "Guess you have some spine after all, boy."

"Do you understand me?"

Hollister gave another wheezing cough. "You don't need to worry. Your precious Laney is safe from me. Matilda didn't steal that money."

Dalton straightened. "You knew about the money?"

"Course I did. I gave it to her."

"You? You gave her almost a million dollars?" Generosity did not seem like Hollister's style.

"When she found out she had Alzheimer's—" again he paused to cough "—she came to me. Said she knew things, so I paid her off. She didn't steal the money. She blackmailed me for it."

For a moment Dalton's mind raced. Then he leaned forward again and said, "The threat still stands. If you—"

"Damn, boy, calm down. I'm not going after Matilda or that girl of hers. Far as I'm concerned, Matilda earned that money. She figured out what no one else did. Took a hell of a lot of courage to blackmail a man like me. Can't help but respect that."

It figured. His father had never respected him. A lifetime of good decision-making, years of smart business leadership and millions in profit hadn't earned his father's respect, but blackmail did.

Dalton walked out of his parents' house without saying another word to either of them. He was done there.

Fourteen

There had been a time in her life when she'd run fast and far from her problems. This situation with Dalton was exactly the kind of thing that would have had her calling U-Haul. But she wasn't eighteen anymore. She had a job, kids who depended on her and more belongings than could fit in her hatchback. Besides, she had Gran.

Even if she wanted to bolt, even if everything else in her life was stuff she could walk away from, Gran needed her, so Laney would never leave.

So she was stuck here in Houston—within shouting distance of Dalton. Still driving his car for God's sake.

At least she had her keys back—he'd had her purse couriered over just that morning, but since her car was still stuck downtown at his office, she'd had to drive his Lexus to school. Like she didn't have enough stress in her life without spending the day worrying that his car was going to be dinged in the school parking lot.

When she walked out of the school at five-thirty, she felt a wave of relief that the cream Lexus was still where she'd left it. It was followed immediately by a wash of panic, though, because her bright red clunker was parked next to it.

She scrounged in her purse and pulled out her house keys. She thumbed through them, cursing. He'd obviously taken her car keys off before returning her bag. Why did she always feel one step behind in her dealings with him?

Well, at least one problem was solved. She no longer had to worry about how to get her car back, but like a damn Hydra, five other problems sprouted up. She didn't want to see Dalton again this soon. She so didn't have the strength to push him away again today. She was terrified he'd say the word and she'd rush back into his arms.

The driver's side door of her car opened up, and Dalton climbed out.

Instead of the business suit that she'd expect a CEO to be wearing on a Tuesday afternoon, he was dressed in jeans and a gray T-shirt. The things that man did for jeans should be illegal. And here she'd thought he looked good in a suit.

Unfortunately, she only had a moment to enjoy the view before she noticed his expression. His eyes were narrowed, his jaw clenched. His hands were shoved deep in his pockets, accentuating the lines of tension in his shoulders.

Okay. So she clearly didn't have to worry about him begging her to come back to him. Scratch one problem off her list.

Her steps slowed as she approached him, stopping a good five feet away from her car. When he didn't immediately offer up her keys or extend his hand for hers, she molded her lips into a sort of smile and said, "Um…hi?"

"Tell me about your grandmother's finances."

The bottom dropped out of her stomach. Her time with Dalton always felt like a roller coaster—all swooping highs and plunging depths. But this went straight past the grand roller coasters she'd loved as a teen to the Tower of Terror's thirteen-story straight drop with no warning.

He didn't even give her a moment to muster her defenses. "Don't pretend you don't know what I'm talking about."

She propped a hand on one hip. "If you know what I know, then there's no point in my telling you."

"Nice try, but I want to hear it from your mouth."

"Fine. My grandmother's finances are…complicated." His gaze narrowed, and he looked like he wanted to leap across the distance between them and strangle her for dodging the question. "Okay, okay. They're…a tangled mess of crap."

"Because…" He trailed off, and she knew he was giving her one last chance to offer any explanation.

"Because she clearly had money she'd been trying to hide." She blew out a breath. "Look, I know where you're going with this."

"Oh, now all of a sudden you know?"

She slanted him a look under her lashes, suddenly feeling defiant. "You wanna be self-righteous, or you wanna let me tell you what I know?"

He pressed his lips into a firm line and nodded.

Laney came closer and propped her butt against the side of her car beside him. "I got power of attorney for Gran last year."

"Only last year?"

Laney ducked her head to dig around in her bag—not for anything in particular but to avoid meeting his gaze. She knew what he was thinking and did not want him to see her embarrassment. Because, yeah, she knew it was ridiculous that Gran had clung so fiercely to the last shreds of legal control she had over her life. At first, Laney had figured it was normal. People didn't want to admit how far gone they were. But then Gran had come right out and told Laney she didn't trust her with her money. She would never trust her with her money. That had stung.

"Yeah. Last year." She pulled out her lip gloss and smeared it on. "First couple of months was just sorting through documents, finding accounts, doing paperwork. It wasn't until the spring that I noticed there was something wonky with her money."

"Wonky?"

"Yes, wonky. That's a technical term we teachers use. It's for when someone should be poor but isn't. And trust me, we teachers know a lot about how to be poor. We teachers know that no matter how careful you are with your money and no matter how well you invest, a working-class salary doesn't turn into millions overnight."

"Okay, so you'd noticed her finances were wonky, but you didn't think to mention it?"

"Mention it?" She waved a hand in frustration. "Who was I supposed to mention it to? Should I have gone to your mother? Should I have contacted the police? The FBI? Gran can barely function. What good would mentioning it do? I couldn't even touch the money. Five years ago, when she was first diagnosed—which was right about the time her wealth suddenly increased tenfold—she put all her money in a trust. The monthly payments go straight to Restful Hills. I can't do anything else with the money even if I wanted to. Besides which, without what she stole from your parents, she couldn't afford to live in Restful Hills."

"Stole?" he asked.

"Yes. She stole money from your parents. There, are you happy now?" She huffed her exasperation. "Without that money, she'd be—" Laney broke off, shaking her head, because suddenly she almost couldn't talk. "God knows, I don't make enough to pay for her care."

Dalton pushed away from the car and turned to stand in front of her. He reached out and gently tipped her face up to his. "It never occurred to you to mention it to me."

His words were soft, but there was a note of something in his voice. Regret maybe.

Maybe...or perhaps she was just projecting, because she sure had enough regrets for the both of them.

She forced herself to meet his gaze. "We've covered a lot

of ground in the past week, Dalton. But no, it never occurred to me to tell you."

Ducking his head, he blew out a breath and dropped his hand from her chin. "You don't trust me at all, do you?"

"I…" God, how could she even answer that? She'd slept with him. She'd trusted him with her body. Even that was huge for her, because she wasn't the type to casually sleep with men. Even guys she'd dated for months hadn't gotten as far as he had. But there were levels of trust beyond that. There was "hey, can you watch my cat this weekend" trust. There was "here's the key to my house" trust. And somewhere way, way beyond that was "hey, my grandmother is a felon and I trust you not to turn her in" trust.

Right now, she was *maybe* at the watch-my-cat stage. And she didn't even have a cat.

She searched his face for some sign of what he was feeling. "I wanted to tell you," she admitted. "I thought about it. I worried about it. But I never could bring myself to do it. What if I was wrong about you? How could I risk that?" She shrugged. "So if you want to know if I trust you…I don't know how to answer that."

"You don't have to." He took a step back, then shaking his head he walked over to his car. He paused with his hand on the door. "Did you honestly think I was going to run right to the police and turn your grandmother in? Did you honestly think I care so much about the Cain fortune that I'd have charges brought against an eighty-three-year-old woman? I loved your grandmother. She was tough and stern, but you always knew where you stood with her. She was the one stable force in my childhood. And you know what? She didn't even steal the money. She blackmailed Hollister for it. He gave it to her to buy her off. She was never in any danger."

Gran was safe. Laney wanted to feel something about that. Relief. Joy. Something. Instead, all she felt was a bone-deep regret. She'd risked everything to protect Gran and it was all for nothing.

"I wanted to trust you," she said, but the words sounded like a lame excuse, even to her. "But how could I when it could cost Gran everything?"

Dalton said nothing, but just shook his head as he turned toward his car.

"Wait," she called, jogging around the nose of her car.

He spun back around and came toward her. "No. You don't trust. No matter what you thought I might do with the information, you didn't trust me enough to share it. And you know what I think?"

She mutely shook her head.

"I think you offered to help me find the missing heiress just so you could get in my way. You did everything you could to keep me from talking to Matilda. This isn't just a lie of omission. This isn't just something you forgot to mention. You set out to deceive me. But you know what hurts the most?"

"Dalton, I—"

"I think you did it on purpose."

"I would do anything to protect Gran. Surely you must know that."

"No." He shook his head sadly. "That's not what I mean. I think you knew I'd never turn her in, and I think you still did all this. I think you lied because you'd use the truth to push me away if I got too close to you. You weren't protecting her. You were protecting yourself."

He stared at her, waiting for her to say something, but all she could do was shake her head, not in denial but more in surprise.

"You can't deny it, can you?"

"No," she admitted. She hadn't done it consciously. She hadn't done it on purpose, but she suspected that wouldn't matter to him, because she had done it. "Dalton, I don't even know what to say."

"I love you, Laney. I think I've loved you since I was thirteen. I wanted to marry you and have babies with you and grow old with you."

His words knocked the air out of her lungs. She felt their meaning—the sheer force of his will—pressing against her, ready to swallow her whole. She jerked up her palm like she was warding him off. "Don't act like I'm the jerk here for not automatically trusting you. Because, sure, you say all this now, but really? Since you were thirteen? What about Portia? What about your marriage to her? Didn't you also see yourself living your life with her? Having babies and growing old with her?"

"Yes." He nodded. "I did. But with you, I saw myself also being happy. I'm all in here. I wanted to spend the rest of my life with you. Didn't you want that too?"

For the first time, probably the first time ever, she really thought about what she wanted in her life. Hard work and struggling to get by were things she understood. All that other stuff seemed...out of her reach. Well, it was that damn cupcake behind the glass again.

"Do you want a life with me?" Dalton asked her. "Do you want any of those things?"

"I've been on my own since the day I turned eighteen." Her stomach churned as she struggled to put her feelings into words. "I don't even know how to want those things."

She couldn't stand to see the pain on his face, but she had to continue. "Plus, you've cut me out of your life before. You made the decision that was right for Cain Enterprises. You put the company first. You did it then, and you'll do it again now. That's who you are. No matter how you feel about me, I'm never going to be the perfect CEO's wife. Being with me, marrying me, that will never be the right thing for the company. I'm the wild-child girl you play hooky with. I'm not the girl you marry. And you're the guy who does right by his employees. You're not the guy who sails away on the yacht in the middle of the workweek. We got to pretend to be those people for one day, but that's all it was—us playing pretend."

She half expected him to argue with her. Maybe she even wanted that. After all, Dalton was a fighter. That Cain tenacity was infamous. Surely he wouldn't just let her walk away.

But instead, Dalton just stared at her for another heartbeat. Then he cupped her cheek in his hand and dropped a gentle kiss on her mouth. It was sweet and heartfelt. As achingly beautiful as a butterfly landing unexpectedly on your hand. And just as brief.

His kiss tasted like goodbye. And a moment later, he was gone.

The next day, Dalton found Griffin exactly where he expected to find him in the middle of the workday—at his condo.

"Hey," Griffin said as he opened the door, "you're up early."

Naturally, Griffin was still dressed in his pajama bottoms. Glancing into the living room, Dalton could see some sort of soccer game playing on the big-screen TV. A bowl of cereal sat on the table in front of the sofa.

Dalton looked pointedly at his brother's bare feet and bare chest and then at the cereal bowl. "I'm not up early. It's nearly noon."

Griffin leaned back to glance at the clock on the TV, then he scoffed. "It's 11:05 a.m. That's not *nearly noon*. And I've just got back from the Middle East last night." He walked back toward the sofa. "Hey, you want something to eat?"

"No, thank you." He shut the door behind him and followed his brother into the living room.

"You want some coffee?" Griffin asked.

"Yes, please."

Dalton sank down on the end of the sectional, set his briefcase on the floor beside his feet and dropped his head into his hands. He'd had a long and sleepless night debating what to do about Laney. He still wasn't sure the solution he'd come up with was the right one. Seeing his brother relaxing at home in the middle of a workday did little to increase his confidence in the new plan.

He loved his brother, but, damn, they were just so different.

Griffin came out of the kitchen and set a coffee mug down on the table in front of Dalton. "So," he said, clapping his hands together with exaggerated excitement, "what brings big brother D to my humble abode in the middle of the day?"

Dalton reached for the coffee. "I think the real question is why you're not at work in the middle of the day."

"Hey, jet lag's a bitch." Griffin's face spread into a salacious grin that hinted at something more entertaining than jet lag.

His housekeeper obviously hadn't been by in a couple of days. The sofa pillows had been tossed onto the floor. The coffee table sat cockeyed between the two wings of the leather sectional. From the other room came the unmistakable sound of the shower cranking on.

Griffin's smile widened.

"Oh," Dalton said, finally putting together the obvious.

Griffin glanced at the bedroom door and then back at Dalton. For an instant, something like concern flickered across Griffin's face. When he noticed Dalton looking at him, he forced a smile. "Give me a second, will you?"

Dalton nodded. "Take your time."

What the hell? It wasn't like he had anywhere more important to be. Griffin disappeared into the bedroom and presumably into the bathroom beyond. Griffin wasn't the kind of guy who didn't care about much beside his own pleasure, but Dalton got the strange impression something was up. Obviously, Griffin had a woman in his bedroom. No surprise, even for nearly noon on a workday. Griffin had always had a way with the ladies. Charm came as easily to him as finance did to Dalton. But a woman in the bedroom was nothing new for Griffin. He had no reason to care that Dalton knew she was there, unless either she or Griffin wouldn't want Dalton to know she was there. So what was up with that?

Dalton didn't wonder for long. He had enough on his own plate without borrowing Griffin's problems.

A moment later, Griffin came back out, dressed and flipping his car keys in his hand. "Let's go grab some lunch."

"What about your Froot Loops?"

"It's too late in the day for Froot Loops. Besides, they're

soggy by now. Let me take you to this great little Argentin-ean café across the street. Great coffee. Best steak sandwich in town, I swear to God."

Dalton glanced at the bedroom door behind which the mystery woman was hiding. Griffin obviously didn't want him to know who she was. And Dalton wasn't one to pry, so he let himself be led out of the condo. Fifteen minutes later, they were sitting in a booth in the kind of dive restaurant Dalton would never wander into on his own.

Dalton waited until after their coffee had arrived and they'd ordered their food to pick up his briefcase, extract a file and push it across the table toward his brother. He'd clipped a flash drive to the outside of the unassuming manila folder.

"What's this?" Griffin asked.

"Take a look."

Griffin took a sip of his coffee and then flipped open the folder. He sorted through the pages with an unusual seriousness.

After a couple of minutes he looked up. "Your information about the missing heiress?"

Dalton nodded. "Yes. In addition to the paper copies that are in the folder, there's a digital file on the flash drive, and I've emailed a copy to you. Mostly it's just notes I've made or Laney has made, but I'm hoping you'll be able to sort through it and make more progress."

"You want me to take a look at it? Maybe a set of fresh eyes will see something you've missed."

Griffin had always cultivated his reputation as a playboy. His charm, good looks and easygoing nature made his image all too believable. Even Dalton—who knew him well—sometimes forgot that all those qualities hid a razor-sharp mind. What Griffin lacked in ambition he more than made up for in intelligence.

It was that lack of ambition that Dalton would have to overcome today.

Dalton leaned back against his side of the booth and sipped

the coffee. "I'm not asking you for help. I'm just passing on the information. I'm done searching for the heiress myself."

Griffin's gaze jerked up. "You found her? Who is she?"

"No. I didn't find her. I'm done searching."

"I don't..." Griffin flipped through the pages, almost as if he expected the girl's name to leap off the page, proof that Dalton hadn't really lost his mind. Then he dragged his gaze up to Dalton's. "You're done?"

"Done."

"What, you want me to take over? I've got a trip scheduled for next week, but after that—"

Dalton leaned forward and cut off his brother. "I'm done. I'm not looking for her anymore. I'm not jumping through any more of Hollister's damn hoops. I'm out."

"Fine. You need me to handle this then I'll handle it. You know how I feel about Hollister's games. I'll pass on to you whatever I find."

Dalton nearly chuckled. He thought it would be hard to convince Griffin to take over. It never occurred to him it would be so damn hard to make Griffin understand.

"When I say I'm out, I mean I'm out for good. I'm not searching for the Cain heiress. I don't want Hollister's damn prize. I'm stepping down as CEO. I'm passing the torch to you."

"To me?" Griffin dropped the folder like it had caught fire. "I don't want Cain Enterprises."

"Neither do I."

"Of course you do. It's all you've ever wanted. Every—"

"Right. Everything I've ever done has been for the company and what has it got me? Nothing. So this morning I submitted my resignation."

"You what?" Griffin reeled so hard he actually scooted the entire bench seat back a few inches.

"I resigned," Dalton said simply. "I recommended the board name you interim CEO. I can't guarantee they will, but I talked to Hewitt, Sands and Schield personally. They'll be able to sway the others. Now—"

"You quit?"

"I resigned." Dalton sighed, glancing at his watch. This was going to take longer than he'd thought. "Try to keep up."

"You can't quit. Cain Enterprises needs you. More so than ever with Hollister sick."

"I agree. Cain Enterprises needs a strong leader. But you can be that leader just as easily as I can." Dalton knew that Griffin had never wanted to run Cain Enterprises. And he knew that some on the board would balk because Griffin had a reputation for coasting on name and family connections. But Dalton had faith that when the company needed him, Griffin would step up.

"Even if I wanted to, I'm not prepared to be the CEO. I don't—"

"My assistant knows everything that goes on in the office. If there's anything you don't know, she can bring you up to speed. She'll take good care of you."

Griffin made a strangled choking sound that Dalton took to be impending hysteria.

"I don't… You can't…" Griffin shook his head, like a dog trying to free himself from one of those funnel collars. When he couldn't break free of the noose tightening around his neck, he slammed his fist onto the table. "What the hell brought this on? And what on earth are you going to do if you're not the leader of Cain Enterprises?"

"I'm going to win the heart of the woman I love."

Unfortunately, when he showed up at Laney's school, two hours later, he found out she'd called in sick. She'd sent back the paperwork for the donation he'd agreed to make to the Woodland Theater, along with a note saying she could no longer accept his money. He didn't worry until he checked at her house and found she wasn't there either. That's when it occurred to him that Laney Fortino was a runner—the kind of woman who bolted when the going got tough. It didn't get much tougher than this. What did she really have to keep her in Houston? A grandmother who didn't even know her most days and a lover she didn't wholly trust.

If she didn't trust him, it was because he hadn't given her any reason to. He'd destroyed any trust she'd had as a teenager, and they simply hadn't had enough time together as adults. If this was going to work, he had to earn her trust all over again.

He was going to have a damn hard time convincing Laney she was the love of his life if he couldn't find her.

Fifteen

She knew it was cowardly to call in sick, but she did it anyway. She even told herself she had her reasons. Maybe they weren't half-bad.

Yes, she needed to talk to her grandmother, but really, that could have waited.

The real reason—if she was honest with herself—was that she knew if Dalton came looking for her, the first place he'd look was at her school. He knew how completely devoted she was to her students. Yeah, he'd eventually get around to checking at Restful Hills, but she hoped she'd be gone by then.

A few minutes after arriving, she'd called down to Linda and told her that Gran was having a bad day and shouldn't see any visitors. Linda would definitely call up to let Laney know if Dalton arrived. That way, she'd have plenty of warning before she had to see him face-to-face.

One of the orderlies from Restful Hills usually helped Gran eat, bathe and dress in the mornings. There were three or four women who rotated through the shift. By the time Laney arrived, Maggie was helping Gran brush her teeth. Laney told the woman she could go and then helped Matilda finish getting ready. Then she found reruns of *I Love Lucy* on TV and—figuring that show was benign enough—set Gran down in front of it, while Laney got to work searching for clues to the identity of the mysterious Victoria. She didn't bother asking Gran—not yet, anyway. No point in kicking the hornet's nest before she was ready to run for cover.

As the theme music for *I Love Lucy* filled the air, Laney sat down in front of the bookcase under the window. The top shelf was filled with hardcover novels, most of them from the eighties and nineties. Gran had always loved thrillers and had quite a collection of Ludlum and le Carré novels. The bottom shelf housed old photo albums.

Laney was familiar with the pictures in most of them because she'd put them together herself. Gran wasn't the sentimental type, and she didn't have albums from her own childhood or the years of her marriage—certainly none from Laney's childhood.

However, when Laney had first moved back to Houston, Gran's doctor had suggested that photo albums might help Gran remember the people and places of her past. So Laney had scrounged around for every photo she could get her hands on. Gran had several shoe boxes full of old photos. Laney had had a couple as well. Laney had even tracked down her own mother—who'd been nice enough to send a thick envelope containing some snapshots and a carelessly scrawled note reading, "Hope you're well, darling. Chile is great this time of year. Come see me if you're nearby. Love, Mom P.S. I particularly love the one of you by the ocean. It's always been my favorite."

When she'd gotten the photos from her mother—two years ago now—Laney had quickly flipped through them to find the one her mother mentioned. The only picture with water in it at all had been a grainy shot of Gran and a woman Laney had never seen before, with a fragile-looking blonde girl standing between them—a girl who was most definitely not Laney.

At the time, she'd rolled her eyes, annoyed—but not surprised—that her flighty mother hadn't even known her own daughter well enough to pick her out of a photo. But she was more annoyed with herself for being so excited by the momentary fantasy that her mother would have a favorite photo of her. She'd kept the picture, though, because it was a rare image of her grandmother actually smiling. Laney had guessed the date of the photo based on the quality and color tones of the print and stuck it into the section of the album devoted to that decade. She'd never bothered to ask Gran about the identity of the woman or the girl, and as far as she knew, Gran rarely looked at the albums.

Now Laney pulled the right album from the shelf—she'd carefully labeled each one—and began to flip through. She found the photo about a third of the way into the book. It was exactly as she remembered it. Gran had her hand on the girl's shoulder in a way that seemed both affectionate and protective. Never once had Gran looked at Laney that way. She felt resentment spike through her. She thought she'd buried those feelings long ago, but seeing Gran with another girl, one who had to be close in age to her, only made Gran's repeated rejections sting more.

Laney turned her attention to the other two people in the photo, looking for clues to their identities. The girl wasn't looking at the camera but rather off into space, her expression dreamy. Was this tiny wisp of a girl the missing heiress everyone was searching so hard for?

The other woman in the photo—Laney could only assume she was the girl's mother—was smiling at the camera. But somehow, her expression still looked sad. A little too pinched around the mouth, perhaps. Or maybe it was something in the eyes. Deep-set, long-term regrets.

The longer Laney stared at the woman in the photo, the

more Laney felt as though she'd seen her somewhere before—
that she should recognize her.

Behind her, Gran grumbled something at the TV. Laney
jumped, startled out of her reverie. "What was that?"

"I don't like this show," she groused.

Laney glanced over her shoulder to see Gran sitting with
her arms crossed over her chest, her face twisted into a frown.
"You can change the channel. The remote's right there."

"That Lucy just gets into the same messes over and over
again. Never learns." But Gran didn't change the channel. She
just kept staring at the TV screen.

Looking back down at the photo album, Laney asked, "Do
you mind if I take one of these pictures?"

Gran waved a hand in a "whatever" kind of gesture.

Laney pulled back the magnetic film on the page and
slipped her nail under the corner of the photo, edging around
it until the photo came away from the page. Then she carefully smoothed the clear film back over the other two photos
on the page, both of which were Gran standing with Griffin
Cain in front of an elaborately decorated cake on what must
have been his birthday.

Then Laney flipped back through to the beginning of the
album, comparing the people in the photos to the mystery
woman at the ocean. Three pages in, she found a match. The
picture was of a very pregnant version of the mystery woman.
Whoever she was, Gran had obviously known her for several
years, but that wasn't what surprised Laney. No, what surprised Laney was that the mystery woman had her arm draped
over the shoulders of Laney's own mother.

Both women were pregnant. The photo was taken in the
Cains' backyard, under one of the sprawling oak trees that
Laney had climbed as a girl. Both women were smiling.
Laney's mother had that same carefree beauty she'd always
had. Pregnancy had obviously suited her, even if motherhood
hadn't. The other woman's smile was sad, just as it was in the
later photo. She had circles under her eyes and looked worn.

Laney quickly extracted this photo from the album and then slid the book back on the shelf. She waited until a commercial started, then hit the mute button on the remote and sat beside Gran.

"Can you tell me who this woman is?" She pointed to the photo of the mystery woman when she was pregnant.

"Course I can."

Laney's heart thundered. "Who is she?"

"That whore Suzy." Gran's voice took on a nasty sneer. "God, she was a piece of work. I never could convince my Michael that she was no good for him. She broke his heart when she left him after the baby was born. Took off like some vagabond and left him to take care of her brat. Course he—"

"No, not Suzy." Laney had to swallow her distaste. "The other woman. The blonde."

Gran looked at the picture again, this time taking it from Laney and holding it before her. She frowned, her eyes scanning the picture over and over like she did recognize the person but just couldn't call forth the name. "I don't know her name." Gran's gaze darted up to Laney's. "Why can't I remember her name?"

"Was she a friend of Suzy's?" Because if she had merely been one of Suzy's friends, then she probably wasn't the woman who had written the letter. On the other hand... "Or was she someone you knew?"

"She worked here at the house for a while. Not for long. But—" Gran suddenly gripped Laney's arm "—I should know her. Shouldn't I?"

"No. It's okay." Gran's hand clutched her arm tightly, but Laney kept her own voice calm. "It's fine that you don't know her. I'm sure she's not important."

But in fact, the opposite was true. This woman, whoever she was, had to be very important.

"I never liked *I Love Lucy,*" Gran said again, disapproval thick in her voice as she clenched her hands on her lap. "Lucy never learns her lesson."

"Let me find you something else." Laney grabbed the remote and clicked through the channels until she found a soap opera. Then, she took the photos and her cell phone and closed herself in Gran's bedroom.

A few minutes later, she was on the phone with a resort in Chile. Unfortunately, her mother had already moved on. Laney had known it was a long shot, since the number was two years old. This was what it was like with her mother. Every few years, whenever Laney needed to talk to her, there were hours of phone calls to exotic locations, tracking her down one job to the next. Chile was a bust, but thankfully the person Laney spoke to had kept in touch with Susanna when she started working for a resort in Nicaragua. From there, it was Honduras. And finally she was on to a place in Belize.

After a few hours on the phone and a few more online—thank goodness for Restful Hills wireless—Laney had left a message at a resort where her mother was maybe working as a masseuse. By then it was around lunchtime, so Laney went down to the cafeteria with Gran and watched as Gran ate bland food. She listened with only half an ear as Gran continued to complain about Lucy Ricardo. They were done eating and just letting themselves back into Gran's apartment when Laney's phone rang.

"Hey, honey," her mother cooed when Laney picked up. "It's great to talk to you! Hey, did you get the package of soaps I sent last month?"

"Yeah, sure." Nearly a year ago, her mother had sent a gift pack of herbal soaps. "They were great."

"I have the best new job, honey. And you wouldn't believe it but—"

"Actually I had a question about my childhood."

The line went unexpectedly silent for a second, then finally, Susanna said, "Ah, honey...your father and I, we just didn't work out. I wished I could have—"

"No, it's nothing like that." She'd long ago given up on wishing her mother could be more of a parent. That was a ship that had sailed long ago—sailed right out of the harbor, grazed a reef and sunk to the bottom of the ocean.

"No, Mom. I found an old photo in Gran's pictures. And I'm wondering if you can help me figure out who's in them."

"I don't see how…"

"It's a picture of you in the Cains' backyard." Laney's nerves were jangling just talking to her mother, so she started pacing. "You're pregnant with me, and you're with another woman. She's pregnant too. Do you know who that is?"

Susanna let out a trill of a laugh. "Honey, how am I supposed to remember someone from a picture nearly thirty years ago?"

"Maybe if you saw it!" Laney suggested. "I could scan the photo and email it to you. Do you have an email address?"

"Email?" She said the word like it horrified her. "God, no. This place has no TVs. No computers. It's heaven. You'd—"

"I need you to think, Momma." She walked by the tiny table in the kitchenette where the photo lay. She gave the picture a tap with her finger as she walked past. "It was the summer you and Dad spent in Houston when you were pregnant with me. Was there anyone you knew who was pregnant too? Maybe someone you were friends with? Maybe someone Gran knew?"

"You know, now that you mention it, there was a girl your grandmother knew. She worked for the Cains. At the house. She was Dalton's nanny, I think."

"Do you remember her name? Was it Victoria?"

"No. Something like that, though."

"Veronica?"

"No."

"Violet?" she asked, desperately throwing out names. "Veruca? Velma? Vivian? Ver—"

"Vivian! I think that was it."

"Was it Vivian? Are you sure?" Because she really needed that name. She hadn't realized until now how desperately she wanted to solve this mystery. To find the missing heiress. To find her for Dalton. Because maybe if she could do this one thing for him it would balance out some of the other things she'd done.

"Oh, honey, how could I be sure? That was a long time ago. Decades. Do you know how many people I've met since then?"

Feeling strangely defeated, Laney answered flatly. "No, Momma, I don't know."

"Hundreds. Maybe thousands. When you travel around like I do you meet tons of people. Most of them just drift in and out of your life, and you never think of them again. You know how it is."

"No, I don't, actually."

Frustrated, Laney ended the call a few minutes later after exchanging promises to try to stay in touch better. Promises that Laney knew she'd try to keep and that her mother would forget within hours.

Discouraged, she yanked out one of the chairs and sank onto it, dropping her head into her hands.

Gran shuffled over to stand beside her. From her peripheral vision, Laney saw her grandmother run a finger across the surface of the photo.

Without looking up, Laney muttered, "I don't suppose you know who the girl in that photo is."

"Of course I do."

Laney's head popped up.

"That's my granddaughter, Laney."

The last of the fight just rushed out of her. Why was she doing this? Why was she fighting so hard to find this mystery woman?

Even Dalton didn't seem half as invested in finding the heiress as she was. And his entire future rested on finding the girl. Why was she so desperate to find her, when it would only end in heartache?

What was going to happen if she did find Vee or Vivian or Victoria or whatever the woman's name was? And what if she was the woman who had written the letter? What if that little girl in the photo was the missing heiress? What would come of all this?

That little girl, whoever she was now that she was all grown up, would be thrust into this world of money and power and corruption. Her life would change overnight and not necessarily for the better.

And Dalton, of course, would get what he'd most wanted all his life. He'd get Cain Enterprises and all it entailed. His life would be back on track after this brief interlude of absurdity. It was the least she could do. Maybe it would make up for how badly things had gone.

Slowly she sat up, rubbing her hands down her face.

Gran still stood beside her, staring at the picture of Susanna and the woman who was maybe Vivian.

"That's not your granddaughter," Laney said slowly.

"Of course it's my granddaughter. You think I don't know my own granddaughter?"

But there was a note of uncertainty in her voice, which meant Laney should probably just let it go, but today she just couldn't. "That's Susanna Pritchard. Your daughter-in-law."

Gran ignored her. "Laney was always just like her mother."

"She got the Fortino nose, but every other cell in her body came straight from Suzy Pritchard," Laney supplied, parroting the words she'd grown up with. "I heard that so many times growing up, I started to believe it. But I don't think I'm anything like her."

Laney pushed herself to her feet, indignation really pumping through her veins now.

"When I found out you needed me back in Houston, I came. I moved back home. And I've been to visit you nearly every day for the past three years. I don't think I'm anything like my mother, because she never would have done that. I don't even think I'm like my father, because he could never face adversity." She turned, paced to the other end of the room and turned back to face Gran, who stood there, watching Laney like she was a stranger who'd somehow wandered into her house. "I think I'm like you. I've stayed and done the hard job, even when it was thankless and frustrating and seemed impossible. Even when it hurt to be here, I've stayed. That's not my mother or my father. That's pure you."

Saying it aloud, Laney realized how true it was. Suddenly, she understood things about herself that she never had before. She wasn't some wild, rebellious, ungrateful brat of a girl. Yes, she was stubborn. And she fought back when she was pushed too hard. That was why she'd butted heads with Gran so often—not because they were so different but because they were so much alike.

Laney's stomach turned over as she considered the idea.

She and her grandmother had so much in common, it was amazing she hadn't seen it before. They were both survivors. They'd both lost so many people they loved. Gran had lost her sister, her husband and her son. She'd pushed away the only person who might have loved her in her old age. Laney had lost her mother, her father and grandmother. Now she was pushing away the person who wanted to love her.

Sure, she admired her grandmother: the strength, the stubbornness, the sheer get-it-doneness. Those were all qualities she'd worked hard to nurture in herself.

But here at the end of her life, Gran was all alone. She'd pushed away the only person who might have cared for her. And Laney had almost made the same mistake. But she was done pushing Dalton away.

Dalton spent three hours sitting in his car across the street from Laney's duplex. He actually considered waiting for her at the school, in case she went by to check on her theater class, but he figured a guy could spend only so long sitting outside a school before someone called the police.

It was nearly 5:00 p.m. when she pulled her little Ford into the spot in front of her house. He climbed out of the car and crossed the street. Laney hadn't gotten out of her car. She'd dropped her head to the steering wheel and sat there like she was either crying or exhausted. He knew how she felt.

He rapped his knuckles on the window, and she jumped in response. She stared for a second, startled and pale-faced, before flinging the door open and throwing herself from the car straight into his arms.

She squeezed him hard for a second before pulling back to shower his chin with kisses.

"Oh, my God, you're here!"

He couldn't help laughing a little as he tried to hold her far enough away to look at her. "Yeah, where'd you think I was?"

"I didn't know! I called Cain Enterprises, but your assistant wouldn't tell me anything. I tried calling your mother, but she just yelled at me. Then I called Griffin, and he told me you'd quit." She socked him in the arm. "How could you quit?"

"I—"

"And then I got all freaked out and drove down to the marina. The guard wouldn't let me in, but I could see the boat slip from the gate and it was empty. And then I—"

"You drove all the way down to the bay looking for me?"

Finally she broke off, blushing as she stepped away from him. She bit down on her lip, giving a sheepish shrug as she shoved her hands into the pockets of her jeans. "I couldn't think where else you might be. And when I didn't see the boat, I mean yacht…"

"What'd you think? That I'd taken off to sail around the world?"

"What was I supposed to think? You'd quit, for God's sake!"

He pulled her back into his arms. This time instead of kissing him, she dropped her head to his shoulder and gave a sigh so deep a little shudder went through her body.

"I was right here, in front of your house, waiting for you to come."

"But the boat—"

"The boat stays in dry dock until I call the marina."

"Oh."

"Now why don't we go inside, and you can tell me why you were so desperate to see me that you went to the marina."

He laced his fingers through hers as they walked up the steps to her duplex and she let them in. Suddenly, she was nervous. All that giddy relief at seeing him gave way to anxiety.

The second the door closed behind him, she tried to step away, but he used his grip on her hand to pull her back to him, and she ended up plastered against his chest.

Before she could protest, he cupped her cheek and lowered his mouth to hers. His kiss was slow and thorough—like he simply couldn't stop kissing her. The world seemed to spin around her as she lost herself in his touch, in the feel and scent of him, in the heady joy of having him so close.

When he finally lifted his mouth, he pressed his forehead to hers and breathed out a shaky sigh. "I hope to God you didn't drive out to the marina just because you'd lost an earring or something, because if you did I'm going to be very disappointed."

"I didn't lose an earring."

He gave a huff of laughter. "And?"

"And?" she asked, feigning innocence.

He lifted his head and gave her a serious look. "This better be the part where you tell me you realized you love me too, and trust me and can't live without me."

She swallowed hard and said, "I love you and can't live without you. I want to be with you. Forever."

"Okay." He stretched out the word as he stepped away from her. "What about that trust thing?"

"I don't know yet." She gave him a winning smile and held up a hand to stave off any protests. "But here's the thing. I've decided it doesn't really matter. I've been thinking a lot about Gran and all the people she's lost and all the people I've lost. I don't want to be like her. I don't want to push you away just because I'm afraid of getting hurt. I want to make this work.

As crazy and as improbable as we seem together, I want to be with you."

And then she was back in his arms again, held so tightly against his chest she almost couldn't breathe. And he was kissing her again. Another long, slow kiss that nearly melted the bottoms off her shoes.

A long time later, when they were wrapped in the blankets on her bed, pillows mounded against the headboard, lights turned down low, she sat up abruptly and turned to face him.

"Oh, and I haven't told you the best part. I found out who Vee is! She was your nanny. And she was even pregnant when she worked for your parents, so it could totally be her!"

He chuckled, tracing a possessive hand across her chest, taking advantage of the way the sheet dropped when she moved. "That's the best part?"

His touch tempted her to abandon the conversation but she made herself pull away from his hand and finish her thought. "Okay. It's a part. Not the best." She gave his hand a playful swat out of the way and lay down across his chest. "But it's exciting, right? That I've found her."

"Exciting isn't the word I'd use for that."

"Be serious!"

He shrugged. "It doesn't matter."

"What?"

He stopped kissing her long enough to look at her, and she saw the seriousness in his gaze. "It doesn't matter who Vee is. Or who the missing heiress is. Like Griffin told you, I resigned from Cain Enterprises."

"You don't really mean that, right?"

"I do."

"It was just, like, a gesture, right? Trying to win me back. Now that you have me..."

"It'd be a pretty meaningless gesture if I changed my mind the moment I'd won you."

"But—"

"I'm done with Cain." He must have realized he wasn't going to distract her, because he rolled her off his chest and propped himself up on his elbow. "I realized that the reason you couldn't trust me is because I'd put Cain Enterprises before you even before I was the CEO. You've never had anyone in your life who put you first. I wanted to be that person for you—even if it meant giving up Cain Enterprises."

She frowned, looking baffled. "But I changed my mind and it doesn't matter to me what you do."

"Don't worry. I won't be unemployed for long. Within ten minutes of sending my resignation to the board, two members had called to talk to me about jobs with other companies they work with."

She rolled her eyes as if unimpressed. "I wasn't worried about you being unemployed, but...you love Cain Enterprises. You're the CEO. That's who you are."

"Then I can be someone else. I can't lead a company I don't believe in, especially not if it costs me the woman I love."

"I would never make you choose between me and Cain."

"You're not making me choose. I am."

"You're serious?"

"Absolutely. From now on, you're the most important thing in my life."

She settled back onto the pillow, feeling a little shell-shocked.

He frowned. "Does that make you nervous?"

She rolled over to face him, and a slow smile spread across her face. "No. This expression isn't nervous, it's amazed. And thankful. I—" She broke off abruptly and threw herself at him, kissing him with a passion he eagerly returned. How had she ever deserved a guy this great?

He ended the kiss and pulled back with evident restraint. "Just so we're clear, I know you've been kind of a vagabond up until now, but—"

She pressed a finger to his lips to cut off his words. "If I've been a vagabond, it's because I didn't have a home. But if I have you, then I have everything I need. If I have you, then I have a home." She hesitated, frowning. What if she'd misread him? "I mean, if that's the direction you were going..."

He choked back a laugh. "Yeah. That is the direction I was going. You cut me off before I could get the big proposal out."

Her eyebrows shot up. "There was going to be a big proposal?"

"There was," he admitted with a grin.

She sat up into a cross-legged position, carefully tucking the sheet under her arms, and looked at him sheepishly. "If I promise to be really quiet and not interrupt again, can I hear the big proposal?"

Humor glistened in his eyes, but there was love there as well. Still, she didn't believe he really had planned a big proposal.

"Hang on for one second," he said. "Close your eyes."

"Okay." She closed her eyes and bit down on her lip, listening to the rustling sounds of his movements. She felt him climb off the bed and move around her tiny bedroom.

"Okay. Open them."

She opened her eyes to see him kneeling beside her side of the bed. He'd put on his jeans, but hadn't buttoned them all the way up. Then she noticed what he was holding. An open ring box.

Inside was a lovely diamond set in a delicate ring.

"Dalton—"

"You deserve more than this," he said. "You deserve music and flowers. You deserve a proposal bigger and more romantic than this. But I've been waiting for you my whole life, Laney, and I don't want to wait any longer to put my ring on your finger. Will you marry me?"

For a long moment, she felt as though she couldn't even breathe. Then, she launched herself at him.

"Yes! Of course I'll marry you." Her lips met his in a kiss full of love and passion.

There would be plenty of time for music and flowers later. But this moment, this was all she needed. Like him, she'd been waiting half her life for Dalton. She was done waiting.

* * * * *

COMING NEXT MONTH from Harlequin Desire®
AVAILABLE OCTOBER 30, 2012

#2191 AN OUTRAGEOUS PROPOSAL
Maureen Child
After a hot affair, an Irish businessman proposes a fake engagement to satisfy his ailing mother. But soon the pretense becomes all too real....

#2192 THE ROGUE'S FORTUNE
The Highest Bidder
Cat Schield
A billionaire playboy adventurer needs to present a family-man image to save the auction house—and he knows just the woman to play the part.

#2193 SECRETS, LIES & LULLABIES
Billionaires and Babies
Heidi Betts
When a baby is left in the boardroom with a note that he's the daddy, this ruthless businessman is determined to find the mother—and make her his.

#2194 CAROSELLI'S CHRISTMAS BABY
The Caroselli Inheritance
Michelle Celmer
A quick marriage, an even quicker divorce and a ten-million-dollar baby turn best friends into so much more.

#2195 MIDNIGHT UNDER THE MISTLETOE
Lone Star Legacy
Sara Orwig
Fiery attraction is the last thing this world-traveling Texas tycoon and homebody secretary want to feel for each other. Will they surrender to their passion for Christmas?

#2196 CALLING ALL THE SHOTS
Matchmakers, Inc.
Katherine Garbera
The tables are turned when the producer and host of a matchmaking reality TV show are reunited for their own matchmaking drama.

HDCNM1012

HARLEQUIN *Blaze*™
red-hot reads

Double your reading pleasure with Harlequin® Blaze™!

2 GREAT NOVELS
SAME GREAT PRICE

As a special treat to you, all Harlequin Blaze books in November will include a new story, plus a classic story by the same author including...

Kate Hoffmann

When Ronan Quinn arrives in Sibleyville, Maine, all he's looking for is a decent job. What he finds instead is a centuries-old curse connected to his family and hostility from all the townsfolk. Only sexy oysterwoman Charlotte Sibley is willing to hire Ronan...and she's about to turn his life upside down.

The Mighty Quinns: Ronan

Look for this new installment of The Mighty Quinns, plus *The Mighty Quinns: Marcus,* the first ever Mighty Quinns book in the same volume!

Available this November wherever books are sold!

HB79723

*Bestselling Harlequin® Blaze™ author Rhonda Nelson
is back with yet another irresistible Man out of Uniform.
Meet Jebb Willington—former ranger, current security
agent and all-around good guy. His assignment—to catch
a thief at an upscale retirement residence. The problem—
he's falling for sexy massage therapist Sophie O'Brien,
the woman he's trying to put behind bars....*

*Read on for a sneak peek at
THE PROFESSIONAL*

Available November 2012 only from Harlequin Blaze.

Oh, hell.

Former ranger Jeb Willingham didn't need extensive
army training to recognize the telltale sound that emerged
roughly ten feet behind him. He was Southern, after all,
and any born-and-bred Georgia boy worth his salt would
recognize the distinct metallic click of a 12-gauge shotgun.
And given the decided assuredness of the action, he knew
whoever had him in their sights was familiar with the gun
and, more important, knew how to use it.

"On your feet, hands where I can see them," she ordered.
He had to hand it to her. Sophie O'Brien was cool as a cu-
cumber. Her voice was steady, not betraying the slightest bit
of fear. Which, irrationally, irritated him. He was a strange
man trespassing on her property—she ought to be afraid,
dammit. Why hadn't she stayed in the house and called 911
like a normal woman?

Oh, right, he thought sarcastically. Because she wasn't
a *normal* woman. She was kind and confident, fiendishly
clever and sexy as hell.

He wanted her.

And the hell of it? Aside from the conflict of interest and the tiny matter of *her name at the top of his suspect list?*

She didn't like him.

"Move," she said again, her voice firmer. "I'd rather not shoot you, but I will if you don't stand up and turn around."

Beautiful, Jeb thought, feeling extraordinarily stupid. He'd been an army ranger, one of the fiercest soldiers among Uncle Sam's finest…and he'd been bested by a massage therapist with an Annie Oakley complex.

With a sigh, he got up and flashed a grin at her. "Evening, Sophie. Your shrubs need mulching."

She gasped, betraying the first bit of surprise. It was ridiculous how much that pleased him. "You?" she breathed. "What the hell are you doing out here?"

He pasted a reassuring look on his face and gestured to the gun still aimed at his chest. "Would you mind lowering your weapon? It's a bit unnerving."

She brought the barrel down until it was aimed directly at his groin. "There," she said, a smirk in her voice. "Feel better?"

Has Jebb finally met his match? Find out in
THE PROFESSIONAL

Available November 2012
wherever Harlequin Blaze books are sold.